NANNY STATE

Martin Knox

NANNY STATE

Martin Knox

First Published – 2024
This edition published 2024 by Novel Ideas
Brisbane, Qld
Australia

The National Library of Australia Cataloguing-in-Publication

Creator: Knox, Martin, author.

Title: Nanny State

ISBN: 978-1-7636472-2-0

Subjects: Political philosophy fiction
             Fiction

Typeset in Times New Roman 12pt by Donna Munro Graphic Design.
Cover artwork by Donna Munro Graphic Design.
Printed and bound in Australia by Ingram Spark.
Copyright © Martin Knox 2024
Publisher: Novel Ideas, West End, Brisbane.
htttps://www.martinknox.com
martinknx46@gmail.com

Contents

CHARACTERS

Narrator – Paul Finething
Julia – Paul's partner, Family Court judge
Paul's daughter – Michelle
Michelle's partner – Chance
Michelle's daughter – Andrea
Michelle's foster daughter – Elaine
Nelson – Paul's fellow teacher
Anton – sailing friend of Paul's.
Barker – state parliamentarian

MARTIN KNOX BOOKS

Available from Amazon in Australia, USA, UK and Canada

The Grass is Always Browner (2011)
Love Straddle (2014)
Presumed Dead (2018)
$hort of Love (2019)
Time is Gold (2020)
Animal Farm 2 (2021)
Turkeys not Bees (2022)
Brisbane River Anti-Memoir (2023)
The Camel, The Lion and The Child (2024)
Energy Lessons (2024)
Nanny State (2024)

A few passages have been extracted from previous
books and included in this book without referencing

DEDICATION

I dedicate this book to
my family: Zoe, Tessa, Amani, Uly and Dorian

Acknowledgements

I am indebted to the following.

Donna Munro has looked after the formatting, cover design and publishing.

Dave Jones provided valuable feedback on political matters.

Brad Ahern provided insights into the nanny state.

In the 'Matters Arising' group at Brisbane's University of the Third Age, the nanny state topic stimulated discussion and perceptions.

Sunnybank Hills Writing Group read and discussed my short story Is Australia a Nanny State? This became the foundation of this book.

Author Bio

Martin Knox grew up on a farm in Somerset, England. He rode a horse and played rugby. He graduated as a chemical engineer from Birmingham University. His work with energy was in a nuclear power station, in petroleum engineering in Canada, in coal mine development and in transportation. He researched alternative systems of government at Imperial College, London. He became a high school teacher and wrote science textbooks with energy emphasis, published by the Queensland Department of Education.

This book is his tenth book published. He has been writing fiction and satirical novels full-time since 2013: speculative, love, politics, crime, sport, totalitarianism, science and technology. He is involved in public policy-making, has proposed an underground railway for Brisbane, developed ideas for mitigating flooding of the Brisbane River and an anti-memoir of his spiritual enlightenment following Friedrich Nietzsche. He has written about the philosophy of climate science from a phenomenological viewpoint. He discusses current issues at U3A and has studied philosophy with students at the University of Queensland. He attends community development forums.

He blogs ideas from his books and relates them to events in the news. He writes letters, plays the guitar, plays chess and walks in the park by the river where he lives.

He reads classical novels, watches movies and enjoys The Big Bang Theory.

He is divorced with children and grandchildren.

Chapter 1 Private School

Paul was living in Brisbane when his youngest daughter, 46, unmarried, arrived from a Pacific island with her two girls, Andrea 12 and Elaine 16. Michelle had worked there for an international organisation, advising the government. Andrea had attended the international school and loved riding horses. Michelle had fostered Elaine, from a troubled family on the island. Now the two girls had come with Michelle to live in an apartment in the same building where Paul had lived for 20 years.

Paul's careers had been engineering and teaching. Since retiring he had written fictional stories. When he had a novel idea, usually science or philosophy, he would write it into a story.

'Do you like living here, Dad?' Michelle asked him.

'I do,' Paul replied. 'My apartment is a bit too close to the river when it floods, but your apartment is higher and ideal.'

Michelle's apartment was on the second floor, whereas his was on the ground floor.

He was in a discussion with Andrea and her mother of what school to send her to. She could go to a private school, or to a state school.

'Private school students can be snobbish,' Paul said.

'How is that a problem?' asked Michelle, asserting her independent perspective as usual.

'State schools often have limited funds, which can result in inferior learning experiences and equipment, with less attractive social events,' he said, 'For example, a state school may not have musical instrument tuition.'

'I'm sure Andrea will have plenty she can do,' said Michelle. 'Snobs have an exaggerated respect for high social position or wealth, seeking to associate with social superiors and looking down on those they regard as socially inferior.'

'They cultivate superiority,' Paul said.

'Yes. That's where the nanny state idea comes in,' said Michelle. 'It's a put-down.'

'I'm not sure it is always a put-down,' he said. 'The upper classes have nannies and it's enviable.'

'Australia's classes are less defined than in the UK,' said Michelle. 'Anyway, if others see themselves as socially superior, does it matter?'

'Private school students can learn prejudice that will rebound against them,' he said. 'It could affect who they befriend and who they marry.'

'A private school mother could be a snob and want a lawyer as a son-in-law,' Michelle said.

'Is there any harm in that?' he asked.

'None, if her daughter finds a lawyer who is a good person and she never meets a goth boy in a state school,' Michelle said. 'Her life could be better.'

'Andrea could encounter snobbery and racial prejudice whatever school she goes to,' Paul said. Andrea's father was African. She hadn't seen him for years. Her inheritance was evident from her dark skin colour.

'She's unusual looking,' said Michelle. 'There could be some bullying attempts at school, but she can deal with that.'

'It's a bit early to fix who Andrea should marry,' he said. 'It might be a woman.'

'She's not going to a girls' school,' Michelle said.

'Private schools offer a more exclusive social experience, especially if they take boarders.'

'Andrea can have an exclusive social experience living at home,' Michelle said.

'If she goes to a state school, you would be more involved with her education.'

'I would like that,' she said.

'So would I,' Paul said.

They stopped there to have dinner.

Chapter 2 Nanny State

After dinner, Paul resumed his discussion with Michelle as he helped clear the dishes.

'Private school people talk down state schools as 'nanny state', as if students are not entitled to an equivalent education because they are publicly funded,' he said. 'Private schools are usually better funded, receiving fees from parents and state subsidies. In the eyes of the public, private school students, being self-funded, deserve the best.'

'Because their schooling is independently funded?'

'Yes, because they are not nanny state.'

'Nanny state' is a term of British origin that conveys a view that a government or its policies cater for the masses with unworthy provision that is overprotective, or interferes unduly with personal choice,' Paul said. 'As used in England, the term is a middle or upper class put down of second-rate provision for the lower classes. Education of the upper class is supposed to be independent, tough and character-forming, whereas nanny state conditions are assumed to be less demanding, soft and common.'

'Is that why you don't like the nanny state?' asked Michelle. 'Are you prejudiced against the lower class?'

'The nanny state doesn't offer elite education,' he said. 'Nanny state conditions in education provide for marginalised kids. The students don't feel special or even individual. The term 'nanny' reminds me of The Sound of Music.'

'But Julie Andrews was an upper-class nanny, looking after elite children. She demanded they perform drama and music. It was a good education, wasn't it?'

'Yes and no,' Paul replied. 'They were valued and respected as individuals, but they didn't learn much for themselves. The nanny took control. A nanny does not forge independent strong learners. They become dependent on her as she rules the group. Their father treated them like automatons. The Von Trap family had invisible bonds holding them, that would keep them dependent on their nanny and on each other. They would be greater as a family if they amalgamated, like different metals combine in an alloy, retaining individual qualities and expressing individual ingredients as part of the whole.'

'You seem to resent the weakness in children that makes a nanny necessary.'

'I believe in autonomy and despise collaboration,' he said. 'I value things separately and in assemblies of separate parts. I have no interest in merging entities except when they owe allegiance to a common ancestor or school.'

'Why not?'

'Individuals are like tools,' he said. 'Each one is a phenomenon having its own purpose. A spade cannot do the work of a shovel, nor can a shovel be a spade. They are different and no synthesis of the two can be as useful as when they are used separately.

'Doesn't that limit the individual?' Michelle said.

'When an individual joins a team, it can be great,' he said. 'The unity a nanny brings is artificial and temporary.'

'A nanny is better than nothing,' said Michelle. 'It sounds as though you don't approve of nannies?'

'Not permanently,' Paul said. 'We have what they call a 'nanny state.' It has the appearance of protecting vulnerable individuals from bullies, who would grab more than they should, like a nanny who controls greedy unruly children and gradually takes over. It is not a permanent solution.'

'I appreciate a nanny state, when it relieves me of parenting duties, which for a single parent are relentless and lonely,' Michelle said. 'There is a constant demand for my time in childcare, driving car pools to youth groups, to sports and to after-school activities. It's constant and it's lonely. I need all the nanny state help I can get.'

'Schools can offer a great deal of childcare but childcare has to be paid for,' he said.

'Are there any fee-paying schools that receive state funding?' she asked.

'Plenty. Every suburb has ordinary state schools and one or two private schools that are partly self-funded,' he said. 'The two types of school are different. The nanny state wants all schools to be egalitarian but the better funded private schools set a high standard for them to match. The state schools are unable to compete in academic performance with the private school children whose group performance is boosted by students on scholarships. In private schools, parents have higher expectations and want the students to be disciplined. The teachers have to be more autocratic. These schools are not exclusive and have fees paid depending on what can be afforded, or obtained on a scholarship. There are several private schools accessible from here and also elite schools with exorbitant fees. They offer choice, rather than endemic privilege.'

'How did education become so variegated?' Michelle asked.

'There are two types of school: State and privileged,' he said. 'Competition has created schools with different education standards. If you want more, you can get it if you choose to pay for it.'

'It makes a nonsense of equality of opportunity,' said Michelle.

'There are differences in outcome,' Paul said. 'Outcomes are not equal. Private school results are boosted by subsidising high performers with scholarships. The coaching benefit is shared with other students.'

'Then everyone is better off,' said Michelle.

Paul wasn't so sure. He had worked in schools where students were streamed. He was not comfortable with segregating young students by ability. No student wants to be put in a second or third rate class. The nanny could give a false impression that they should strive to improve only deficient skills, rather than all their skills.

'At a private school, Andrea will be under more pressure to learn because you will be paying fees, but at a state school she will have more autonomy and could perform equally,' Paul said.

'If it's pressure versus autonomy, Andrea will respond best to autonomy,' Michelle said.

Chapter 3 State School

Near our home was a State high school with a very good academic reputation. Paul and Michelle reviewed the school's provision of a safe environment. It had a good safety record. Public schools are often in lower socioeconomic areas and neighbourhood gang violence and drug culture can spill over into the school, during and after hours. The State tries to protect school children with locked gates, limited access, security cameras, patrols and police presence. Such provision usually follows incidents. The school teachers actively 'nanny' the students, routinely providing protection.

'I think Andrea will be happiest at the state high school,' said Michelle.

Paul agreed. 'I expect her to do well.'

Andrea started at the school. She had a wide range of subject choices and engaged keenly. She was used to a more relaxed curriculum and sometimes yearned for more freedom to socialize with the other students.

'Make friends with a couple of high-performing students,' Paul advised Andrea. 'Copying others' homework is a good way to catch up.'

'Wouldn't it be better if she did the homework herself?' said Michelle.

'We can't expect her to catch up all at once,' Paul said.

Elaine's school history was chequered and because her family lived away, she was restricted to a state funded teen college, where she would develop vocational skills. Hopefully both girls would adapt to their schools' cultures and become well-rounded students. Elaine would do well to blend in and forget the bad times at her previous home on the island.

When they felt unwell, both girls took days off school. Their schools did not impose fines for absence as do some secondary schools in England. Nor did they require students to purchase insurance for accidents and losses of equipment as in France. Students could take their mobile phones to school, but had to leave them in lockers for use during breaks. Students were free to attend school when they wanted

Their travel to school on free council buses involved only a short healthy walk. The buses were not fitted with seat belts. When it rained, Andrea asked her mother to take her in her car. Michelle took care of both girls wonderfully well. Michelle was used to dealing with people and related well to teachers and others responsible for the girls.

When they were sick, Michelle wanted them to see a doctor.

'What's the medical system here? Is it 'nanny state' like the NHS? I hope so,' she said.

We had lived in England for several years. The British National Health Service was a source of national pride. Specialists and treatments were free for everyone without long waiting times.

'In the UK, you can 'go private' with your own hospital room and personal doctor,' said Michelle.

'It's similar here,' Paul said. 'The national insurance scheme is called Medicare and it pays for most things. You can pay for specialists, like in the NHS. Dentistry isn't covered though.'

'Why not?'

'Dental treatments have alternatives with a range of costs. The patient has to decide how much they can afford.'

Andrea was keen on basketball and she joined a club. She got up at 4 am to train at rowing on the river. The training and conditions were arduous and she bonded with her team members. She met girls who became friends and she visited their homes.

The school did not seem to suffer from the 'second-rate' reputation applied to state schools. Andrea had a wide range of choices of activity. Students were under-pressure to perform but there were alternatives for low achievers. It seemed that the focus was on the top students, although there was some remediation for those struggling. Neither Andrea nor Elaine were academically inclined and they often required Michelle's help with homework.

Paul worried that Andrea was coasting at school, without seeming to strive.

'She has plenty of time yet to distinguish herself,' Michelle said. 'She will find her way through.'

'The world wants young people who are self-starters,' Paul said. 'I have heard good training requires a willingness to work and accept correction. Those who wait, fall into things and don't get very far.'

'There are many ways to get started,' said Michelle.

When the weeks became terms, Andrea began to achieve well.

'Academic achievement isn't the be all and end all,' said Michelle. 'It takes more than that to be a good person. I don't know what she needs, but she is trying hard at basketball and rowing.'

'Now that she is striving at something, I am reassured, but where will sport take her?' Paul asked.

Andrea often was out of class at sporting competitions. Paul wanted to know the school's philosophy for sporting achievement. Andrea had to catch up when she missed lessons to go to sport.

The nanny policy at her school controlled students from developing bad habits. Alcohol, cigarettes and vaping were prohibited. There were regulations requiring the school to sell healthy food and drinks. The regulations supposed that denying students access would reduce consumption of prohibited items. Students arriving at and leaving school were protected. School lunches were regulated.

Paul was sceptical of the value of surrounding the school with road crossing superintendents, because students did not learn to cross cautiously. This was over-protection.

Although both girls struggled at times, they were not singled out for remediation. There was special provision for any students disabled by ADHD, dyslexia and autism.

The protection of Andrea at school was impressive and her 'nanny state' school was in an academic class of its own.

Elaine was older and settled into regular school work. Both girls were doing well.

Chapter 4 Studying

Andrea often talked on her phone with school friends and went out with them. Paul was reminded of her mother at the same age, at a state school.

'Should I be good at school, or at home?' Michelle had asked them.

'At school,' her parents said.

It was a choice Michelle answered by throwing herself into her schoolwork. Recognising this, they had not subjected her to a regimen that was oppressive at home. She was wilful and did more or less as she liked. At school, she pleased her teachers and won awards.

Now Andrea was doing as she liked and making an effort at schoolwork, Paul worried where this was taking her because he seldom saw her, although she lived next door.

Her home was her refuge, where peace and sustenance could be found, with space to pursue her own interests, when shelter from the outside world was wanted, especially at night and in bad weather. She expected her mother to also provide foods she liked and money for various declared and undeclared purposes. At other times, home was a base to equip expeditions with food and clothing, gaining morale needed to take risks.

Home was a place under parental control. Andrea's school took a nanny role in expecting parents to equip their students, providing nourishing lunches and arriving at school on time. Andrea had a serious interest in basketball, attending obligatory training after school on most days.

Elaine's school allowed her to pursue a vocational interest in salon cosmetics by day release. The girls wouldn't be nannied, choosing their best lives for themselves expecting their mother to provide shelter and money, as their rights.

The schools set homework to consolidate classroom learning and for independent practice. Homework guidelines were flexible, with parental support varying between parents. Parents often intervened in homework tasks set by teachers, who regarded homework as an opportunity to apply nanny state conditioning.

The girls also pursued other interests outside school, in community run sports and social clubs. They had opportunities to interact with strangers outside the sheltered school environment and made good friends.

The two girls were young teenagers and required supervision to stay on the straight and narrow. Never before did Paul live close by youngsters of this age. They made demands that Paul thought were inappropriate for their age. For example, Andrea phoned her friends whenever she had the opportunity. She had used digital technology and social media from an early age and she seemed to be spending too much time on her phone. The government had announced plans to ban children from social media but it might be difficult to implement because the conflict seemed to be generational rather than technological.

Andrea's friends included a boy she phoned frequently, who she referred to as 'my boyfriend.' There were no guidelines or models of inter-gender correspondence and it worried Paul that she spent so much time talking with him and going to the movies. She was only 12 and he worried that their interaction would become increasingly physical, straying into illegal promiscuity. She watched movies where juicy sex was commonplace, thinly disguised.

His impression of the girls at home was that they would spend their time on their phones, or watching television, unless prevented. When reminded several times by their mother they would pore over their laptops and claim to have finished homework tasks. They seldom mentioned what these tasks were and their explanations were mumbled jargon and unintelligible to him. Their school work was lower priority for them than watching movies. The movies they watched seemed often to be violent, failing to show genteel aspects of life. Due to frequent absences from school, they could not expect teachers to take much interest in their progress.

Soon Andrea would be old enough to have inalienable rights of pursuing life's basic necessities, of enjoying and defending her life and liberties, of acquiring, possessing and protecting property and of seeking her own safety, health and happiness, in lawful ways.

There was censorship of movies and television series, but little was left to the youngsters' imaginations. What Paul wanted for them was a grounding in how to avoid the physical behaviours in sexual relations, warning of consequences and how to avoid problems.

Andrea and Elaine were absent from school quite often. This did not seem to be a big deal with the school, or with friends, who often stayed away too.

Paul was told one day their lounge at home was a 'sick room', but he wasn't told of any medical complaint. Their illnesses seemed vague, possibly faked, he thought. When they were sick, they watched television. He wrote to Michelle reminding her that their 'sick room' did not seem appropriate for the girls to make a recovery: they were allowed to have visitors; eat junk foods and soft drinks; access social media; and watch TV. They seldom exercised, except at sport. They seemed to enjoy being 'sick' in comfort.

Their sickness should in his experience require bed rest recovery, resuming their daily routines without undue delay.

Michelle told him it was none of his business and the sick girls' behaviour was satisfactory.

Underlying his complaint was that the girls and their mother didn't have enough time for him. They were polite enough when their paths crossed but they didn't come to see him or enable him to visit them. When he did go to see them, they would put the television on, or go to their rooms, or talk on their phones. This was disappointing. When he tried to have a serious discussion with them, they were without experience of presenting arguments. They were his only family in Australia and being so ignored was painful.

The girls' conversation with him was stilted and without genuine interest. His own conversation with them didn't get very far, partly because often he didn't understand what they said. But the overriding problem was mutual lack of interest from lack of respect. They didn't seem to recognise it as a problem, as if they hoped he would shut up and go away or die. They liked to joke about his impending death and what he should do with his money.

Their idea for his money was that he should spend it on indulgences. Her purchases bought for them gimmicks, processed foods and ice cream. All he could do was wait, hoping they would become friendlier and more frugal.

Provision for Andrea to pursue her own freedom was good. The apartment was comfortable, well-equipped and safe. She would be protected in a fire by smoke alarms and fire-proof doors. She had been vaccinated against polio, meningitis, tetanus, TB and Covid. During the epidemic she had been quarantined and had worn masks. The building and grounds had periodic safety inspections which reduced hazards and improved escape routes. If residents had weapons, he had not seen them. Noisy parties were held by neighbours at reasonable times. Residents' dogs were noisy and dangerous when passing on stairways. In a flood, they would have to evacuate before the water cut off the escape route.

Andrea had become used to living there protected by rules and traditions.

When Paul asked her how she was getting on at school, she invariably replied 'Not good. I'm bored.'

Michelle acknowledged Andrea's learning difficulty, speaking up on her behalf.

'The school is authorised to care for the kids, not to bore them rigid with learning they don't understand. She knows what is best for her and the school can't proceed as if her wants don't matter.

He was shocked that Michelle condoned what he regarded as a lack of discipline. He regarded education as a process of reinforcement by rewards and punishments.

'The curriculum has been approved by parliament,' he said. 'Of course it's boring.'

So much of his training had been boring, he couldn't imagine any other way. Peers who had done what they liked had always failed, crashed and disappeared. He hoped Andrea would not fail.

'They shouldn't have a curriculum,' said Michelle. 'Rousseau in about 1789 proposed that education of children was unnecessary and children should be able to do what they liked.'

'He thought kids were perfect and didn't need to be moulded,' Paul said. 'Not many parents believe that today.'

'State education has come to mean a lot more than it did in Rousseau's day,' said Michelle.

'You're right,' he said. 'A nanny state has taken over. Schools should be able to teach subjects that match their teachers' experiences. The community would be strongest if students are exposed to a variety of teaching styles. The national curriculum is totalitarian and offers a narrow range of experiences. It is a harmful nanny state policy, to control students rather than educate them. Homogeneous curricula are harmful.'

'It does allow children to change schools with less difficulty,' Michelle said.

'You mean it is easy for them to quit?'

'That is a small issue: the tail shouldn't wag the dog,' said Michelle.

Michelle liked the homogeneity of state schooling. She had enjoyed her secondary schooling.

'I met all kinds of kids she said. As a result I now get on with a wide range of types, even snobs.'

She thought her career had not been held back by her state schooling. Some of her peers had gone to elite schools and she was still in contact with them.

Paul was careful not to openly criticise state schooling. He had taught at a state school and although the learning lacked sophistication, it was robust. Andrea liked her school and was doing well with their support. But his politics had taken a turn to the right and he had become generally sceptical of the nanny state's ability to inspire thinking and debating skills..

Chapter 5 Community

Paul lived in West End, Brisbane, a suburb where Bohemian tastes limited development of cosmopolitan culture. Most of the state laws regulating health and safety were reasonable. He had protested lack of bicycle lanes, excessive speed limits and excessive heights of apartment buildings. The City Council responded minimally.

Michelle and the girls had been living happily in their apartment since moving in. The apartments met nanny state regulations, ensuring safety and comfort. West End suburb had ample roads and a variety of amenities. Buildings had metal roofs of the standard accepted locally to resist cyclones. The apartments were attractive in appearance, with strong balconies and cladding of a type that would resist fire.

Paul was a member of a local community group concerned with development of West End. The members of the group were local people employed in the City or operating small businesses.

City planners wanted to turn the suburb into a dormitory for workers and students. They predicted that West End would have the fastest growth in the city and they approved building of forests of high-rise apartment buildings. It seemed that the government was favouring development to reap a rates bonanza. There was a frenzy of building. Paul wanted West End to be stable, with growth of family accommodation, potential for small businesses and amenities.

The nanny state intervened in development of West End with building regulations and operating standards. These concerned among other things, building heights, environmental health, food safety, infection control, occupational health, public and road safety.

Paul was concerned that although many of the hundreds of regulations were common sense, fire, smoke alarm and safety regulations were excessive and a burden to residents. Maintaining the safety systems was expensive.

'The regulations do reduce accidents,' he acknowledged. 'West End is a safe place to live, with above average longevity. The nanny state regulations impose a higher standard of living than many people can afford.'

The nanny state provided West End people with a wide range of services. Immigrants and asylum seekers could obtain help from the government, such as language coaching and accommodation. Homeless people could receive assistance with rent control, rent subsidies and housing from the government. Disabled persons could receive care and other benefits, free under the National Disability Insurance Scheme. Paul was concerned that benefits available to immigrants exceeded those available to local residents. The most popular state services were infrastructure and transport, enabling residents to participate in the local economy. Access to supermarkets, transport and facilities was made easier with age concessions such for bus travel.

The girls went out and about town, to school, shopping and to events at friends' places. The nanny state protected them from exploitation and harmful substances such as alcohol, cigarettes and vapes banned, except under licence. Premises selling foods such as fast foods required licences which depended on inspection. The nutritive content of fast foods was inspected periodically. Food preparation methods used for foreign foods came under close scrutiny and licences were refused for unusual foods.

When the girls went to the beach and fun parks, safety was supervised, with swimming restricted to flagged areas and safe conditions of operation imposed, such as lookouts for sharks.

The nanny state controlled safety. Regulation of vehicles with safety requirements included ignition locks, childproof car door locks, seat belts, speed limits, drink driving, scooter helmets and safer vehicles. Roadworks safety was subject to regulated supervision.

There were State health controls. Mass screening of pap smears, prostate and bowel cancer was voluntary, paid for by the nanny state. Emergency care was freely available in hospitals tests and ambulances were freely available to people without insurance. Medical equipment such as wheelchairs and prostheses were provided free by hospitals.

'You are fortunate to live in a community that is safety conscious, with health care available,' Paul told Andrea and Elaine.

'We are old enough to take care of ourselves,' said Elaine.

'Getting there,' Paul said. 'But you are still too young to be out after dark.'

He was pleased to have nanny state intervention controlling health and safety. However, the restriction of foreign foods prevented development of cosmopolitan culture and limited tourist interest in the community.

All employees were awarded annual leave of 20 days per annum, at full pay.

He wanted regulation against wasteful use of all types of energy. Cost of the energy was not a sufficient deterrent and inefficient technologies persisted in transport, heating, lighting and motors. In his view, wasting of energy in vehicles caused thermal and chemical emissions. The waste was expensive, caused pollution and depleted supplies of mineral resources. It consumed scarce energy resources and was often noisy and anti-social. It was immoral. New white goods had energy efficiency ratings, but road vehicles did not. Room heaters and aircons were unregulated.

The nanny state that had intervened against fossil fuels should intervene against wasteful use of energy. Time-of-day metering could penalize customers for demanding electricity at peak and shoulder times. Because power generation by solar panels was sensitive to times of intense solar energy, electricity sales metering should take the weather into account.

When a person buys a single bar infrared room heater, they could pay $100 for a 1 kilowatt appliance, but if they use it on only a single occasion, on the coldest day of the year, for an hour, the person could pay only 35 cents for 1 kWh of electricity, but the cost of a 1kW large gas turbine needed for peak supply could be $1000/kW. The supplier paid ten times more. It could be less if there was spare generator capacity already installed, but the power supplier could black out a neighbourhood with a supply failure. Blackouts had occurred and more were expected.

Rationalisation of electricity charges by user demands, such as time of day and weather, could be objective or arbitrary. If a pensioner's single bar heater would be so expensive that they wouldn't use it, it was a moral judgement for the Electricity Authority to decide what part of the cost to charge to other users, allowing them to avoid temperature extremes. By allowing the heater to be used, an aged person could be saved from freezing. Hardship in the mild climate was unlikely, but a nanny state could negotiate a fair tariff schedule.

Chapter 6 Morality

Paul was invited to several parties and met Julia, a family court judge and organiser of a campaign to save an iconic heritage building from redevelopment.

'The government is selling Yungaba as a heritage site,' she said. 'This is an example of government over-reach to promote commercial development and we can't ignore it,' she told me. 'There aren't many historic buildings left in Brisbane,' she said bitterly.

'What do you want them to do with it?' he asked.

'We've prepared plans to convert it to an immigration museum, to commemorate the important role of immigrants in our community,' she replied.

'That could be popular with city visitors and school excursions.'

'It would also be popular with the state nanny if she was interested in cultural development,' said Julia. 'It seems she is not.'

'Is your proposal for a thoroughly modern museum?' he asked.

'You could come to our next meeting and judge for yourself.'

He agreed he would go and wrote down the date and time.

Paul asked Julia to his 60th birthday party at his home. She seemed a few years younger.

'Please play something,' she asked, eyeing his guitar standing in a corner.

'Okay, if you will sing,' he said.

His talent was modest but he enjoyed performing when people sang.

Everyone joined in singing Bobby McGhee.

Julia sang the melody well, with great rhythm and perfect pitch, her voice reminding him of Julie Andrews'. Her singing was much better than his.

'Will you teach me the guitar?' she asked after several songs.

She came to his place the following week. She borrowed his old guitar for the lesson. They spent an hour singing and playing together.

For their next lesson a week later, at her place, she had bought a lovely Spanish guitar with nylon strings, like his. He gave her copies of lyrics and chords he had downloaded and they played and sang together.

They played together every week, alternating between her place and his. Whoever was host cooked lunch. He served chicken satay skewers and apple pie. She put on a curry, followed by apple crumble and ice cream.

She learned the guitar quickly. They went out to community events. They became a couple. He went to her Yungaba meetings. Julia came to his political group and it was good to have her input. She seemed genuinely interested in what he called the 'nanny state', which he said was the government trying to help some people without offending others.

'You seem to be a do-gooder,' said Julia.

'I try to get the State to do good,' I said. 'It's what they were elected for.'

'Are you saying that the nanny state is the government being seen to get good things done?' Julia said.

'Yes, that's usually what they're up to. They are a moral force.'

'What drives the nanny state?' she asked.

'The government wants to do things the electorate wants,' I said. 'They can encourage people to work, buy things and pay taxes. They can hand out benefits and cash they have collected as taxes. It's big of them, don't you think? When the nanny state keeps people working and buying things, the nanny can take the credit. They can regulate ownership and use of new technologies. They can take a leading role in constructing infrastructure for people to use. They can claim to be keeping people employed, simply by creating an optimistic investment environment, by handing out public debt and collecting it again.'

'Is the nanny state an arm of government?' asked Julia.

'The government was elected for making promises and winning confidence by promoting themselves,' he said. 'When we call in their promises, they run a mile.'

'Why is there a nanny state?' Julia asked.

'The government members have a duty to serve the public and they are able to self-serve,' Paul said. 'When the government announces a new programme, there can be public approval or disapproval. If they alienate a section of the population, it may not register until votes are counted in the next election. By then it may be too late for change. Consequently, announcements by the nanny state are quite cautious.'

'Do others in your group plan to nominate for the election?' Julia asked.

'I don't know. I prefer to operate alone. I will support others when I like what they're doing.'

'Do you have any proposals that others will back?' she asked.

'I want development of a multicultural community, but immigrants' frustrations with the authorities' biases have caused racial violence. Immigrants could only afford rents in ghettoes ruled by heavy-handed police. I realised that something was wrong in the community and that immigrants could only get leftover jobs, houses and freedoms. It was unfair and my mission has oriented to obtaining fair treatment for them.

'It is shameful that nanny state benefits are subject to racial discrimination. It is illegal but subtle and if elected I would work to bring fair treatment to immigrants.'

'You could be busy,' Julia said.

'Packaging is another problem. The waste dumped on land and in the sea is immoral. I wanted the nanny state to regulate against wasteful packaging of food and other supermarket products. There is too much encasing of products in plastics. These include juice and milk jugs, grocery bags, bread bags, produce bags, and food storage boxes.

'As of April 2023, the sale or supply of items made from single-use plastic such as drinking straws, cutlery, cups, plates, drink stirrers, and polystyrene drink and food containers were prohibited in all Australian States and Territories.

'Food-contact packaging used for food that is not made on premises, i.e. food for retail sale, is excluded from the plastics bans in all States and Territories.

'Consumers are not always able to decline buying packaging when they purchase products. Supermarkets could be required to offer packaging alternatives such as multi-use containers at low cost. Suppliers should not be able to offer offensive types of packaging.

'I agree, something needs to be done about excessive packaging. Retailers are going too slowly. We need someone like you to get parliament's attention.'

'The federal government can only do so much. We count on local authorities and the nanny state to apply environmental regulations. This happened with the change from single-use plastic bags in supermarkets. It could happen with packaging.'

'First the change has to have wide moral acceptance.'

'Images of packaging despoliation of the environment can be adopted by the Spectacle.'

'It won't happen unless someone can make money from it.'

'The nanny state may have to pay advertisers.'

'That could work!'

Chapter 7 Yungaba

Julia was trying to save from development the 200-bed Yungaba Immigration Depot built on Kangaroo Point beside the Brisbane River in 1878. It had accommodated thousands of immigrants arrived by ship from the UK and Europe in a two-storey brick institutional building, designed as an immigrant reception and processing centre, by John James (JJ) Clark, colonial architect for Queensland. Transporting the immigrants to a new life in Australia was a nanny project paid for by State governments. Many were single and there were families too.

From the end of WWI and throughout the 1920s, immigration swelled. The Great Depression of the 1930s led to a rapid fall in numbers, exacerbated by the cancellation of the assisted passage schemes. In 1938 the assistance scheme was reinstated and numbers rapidly climbed, only to fall again with the commencement of WWII.

Yungaba Immigration Depot 1968
Queensland Government, Yungaba Immigration Depot
https://apps.des.qld.gov.au/heritage-register/detail/?id=600245

The elevation of the building was Italianate, Queensland and institutional: Italianate because of the application of enclosing verandahs, developed galvanised iron hoods to the windows and ventilators to the roofs; and institutional because of the resolutely symmetrical treatment. Even the decorative elements were applied with rigid symmetry round the east-west axis. A sturdy segmental loggia sheltered the main axial entry and round arched windows were applied to the twin towers and to the central extremities of the north, west and south ranges.

Kerr, J S <u>Yungaba, A Revised Plan For Its Conservation</u>, Dept of Public Works, Qld, 2001

Although their predecessors had arrived in chains, the immigrants lived there in reasonable comfort while they found their feet in the new land, until offered employment at stations and houses in the hinterland by settlers.

The building served as a hospital in World War II. Afterwards it was used for various purposes but by 2013 it was unoccupied and the State Government sold it for $11 millions to a developer, Lendlease, who drew up plans to build high rise apartments on the site and to convert the building into luxury apartments.

'Yungaba is a part of our history that we should remember,' Julia said indignantly.

'How are you involved with Yungaba?' I asked her.

'We are a group of friends trying to exert moral force for preservation of Yungaba,' she said.

Julia's group were protesting the plan to develop Yungaba and wanted an Immigration Museum, to equal popular immigration museums in Melbourne and Sydney.

The museum project lacked funds, but they hoped donors would get it off the ground if the State Government would reverse the land sale. They began an action in the Environmental Court but before the case could be judged the State Government called it in for State decision and sold the site to a property developer.

We had wanted an 'Immigration World' theme park, with a re-enactment tour following in the steps of immigrants from arrival in a longboat at the jetty, then a welcome speech by a government minister and a simple meal in the dining room, before allocation to dormitories where 'employers' would come and interview them.

There would be museum exhibits of artefacts and garments, with video and audio recordings of the times and a heritage wall with names and lineage of immigrants. It was expected that the museum would become a place where families could gather and celebrate their origins and descent.

The government did not consider renegotiating for a museum, but did require the developer to construct a small multicultural centre. The overall Lendlease plan was to construct 165 apartments and sell them for around $2 millions each, making a huge profit. It was a clever plan that carefully optimised the design for their profit. Designs for the pleasure of apartment occupiers would have cost considerably more.

We learned from the government's lack of response that they would not support our proposed Museum. They had a reflex to decline investment of civic funds in developing culture.

'We can't compete with European history,' a Councillor told me. 'If people want to see history, they should go to Italy.'

The government's role was the opposite of a nanny: it allowed a private interest to exploit public land without adequate recompense. The nanny state was not supposed to profit from Yungaba. Our proposal was to redevelop the site and operate it efficiently for the benefit of Brisbaners. Selling the site for private accommodation was a grab for rates revenue, money that would be swallowed widening roads and disappearing without trace. There were many other sites available for apartment building at Kangaroo Point but there was only one Yungaba. Although the developer conserved the unique architecture, access to the building was limited to owners of the converted apartments, except on one open day each year. The government never considered benefitting the public in a city having few theme parks. It was very disappointing.

The nanny state had served the public badly, giving minimal recognition to the heritage and cultural amenity of the people. Brisbane has destroyed most of its historic buildings. Brisbaners wanted to know their history and an Immigration Museum would be popular for school excursions and family commemoration. It was sad that the City was forging its way into the future without awareness of its past.

The government's heritage committee, its members nominated by the government, silently approved the redevelopment. Valuing our heritage was an important step in developing a healthy community. It was outrageous that a government could sell off a heritage site to its developer friends for a pittance. The nanny state's role was shameful, in mediating the disposal of an asset belonging to the people of Queensland.

Julia had a key to the building and we took Andrea and Elaine for a tour before the place would be shut away from the public.

'This is such a lovely place,' said Andrea. 'I can imagine when they arrived here the immigrants would be thankful and singing.'

'They would be dancing an Irish jig,' Elaine said.

Chapter 8 Economy

A few restored buildings in Brisbane showed places where important citizens had lived and led genteel lives. They were places that reminded that settlers' forebears had been brought in chains and led brutal, short lives.

'I don't think it would have been a good place to be if you were a convict,' said Andrea. 'I read somewhere that if you tried to escape you would be flogged.'

The nanny state had preserved only that part of their history accessed by the middle and upper classes. Ordinary people had crude homes and few possessions and were forgotten. The history of poor folk had almost disappeared.

Records included some details of ordinary lives, telling of manual labour, domestic drudgery and daily preoccupation with survival. History had been written by the survivors and living conditions had been forgotten.

The amount of the City of Brisbane's budget recently exceeded annual expenditure by the nation of Belgium. Expenditure of rates collected from owners of properties was spent largely on projects to relieve congestion on the roads. That expenditure has been largely wasted, because widening of roads and tunnelling had acted mainly to move the location of traffic jams, without reducing vehicle journey times.

The Yungaba protest group was without funds except for donations from group members. I took a lead in briefing a solicitor for our action in the Environment Court. He agreed to work pro bono, but wanted a retainer. I agreed, imagining he would send us an account that we could all share in paying. But he sent it to me alone and the others assumed I would pay it all. I balked. I had the money but that was not the point: there was no reason why I should carry the others. I paid about half and Julia paid the rest. Julia seemed to think that was reasonable. It came between Julia and me, but we moved on to other concerns.

Nanny state expenditure had built car parks, renovated stadiums, redeveloped sportsgrounds, golf courses, theatres and performance venues. Public transport was also being developed. These were nanny projects to benefit the public, generating revenue for businesses and creating employment.

'Public sector spending is propping up the economy,' complained a political leader.

Complainants were not opposed to development itself but debated particular projects.

Nanny state growth and development goals were to impress voters and win votes at State and local elections. The government was expected to authorise projects that would stimulate the economy. The selling of cherished buildings and public land at Yungaba was a mistake, a wrong use of community assets to create expensive apartments and a few jobs.

Proposals said to be 'nanny state', benefited predominately lower social classes. Public festivals united crowds with free events and cheap ice creams. The expenditure on the roads mainly benefited car owners. Sporting and entertainment venues sold expensive tickets. Theatre, opera and ballet had the most expensive tickets, despite nanny state support.

The government sold land in the CBD for a large Development at Queens Wharf. There would be a casino, office accommodation, private apartments, entertainment, shops and a bridge to South Brisbane. The development would benefit mainly wealthy people and the casino could attract criminals. There wasn't much that ordinary people could afford and it would not attract many visitors. Developers depended on amenities to attract customers and a few people who would spend a lot, whereas a nanny state should prefer many people able to spend a little. The Queens Wharf development brought the nanny state into disrepute and magnified the importance of wealthy people.

Chapter 9
Totalitarianism

Paul had tried to understand the meaning of 'Nanny State' in Brisbane. Just when he had figured out how the State Government related to redevelopment of Yungaba, he discovered the State was involved in other arenas where the nanny role was very different.

The McLean family met weekly for Sunday lunch together. After the meal at Paul's place, talk continued in the dining room over coffee. There were Andrea, Elaine, Michelle, Julia and Chance. He was Michelle's man friend from the university. Paul had met Julia recently and it was the first time she had lunched with them.

'State intervention in sport was opposed earlier this week,' said Michelle. 'The referee tried to sideline a player for verbal abuse and he had to back down.'

'What happened?'

'The referee red-carded a player but changed his mind when the crowd booed,' said Andrea.

'How was that opposition to state intervention?' Paul asked.

'The referee was appointed by the State sports authority,' said Chance.

'Why did he change his mind?' asked Michelle.

'Verbal abuse is not against the rules.'

'It should be!' said Andrea.

'It's not a big deal,' said Chance. 'The referee overreacted, is all, a bit of nanny state. The abuse only seemed physical. Bad words are ugly, but not enough to send a player off.'

'It is a big deal,' Paul said. 'It is right to prevent physical abuse but verbal aggression releases strong feelings. It isn't violence and is part of the culture of some sports. It is bad form, that's all. It isn't like blood injuries, when players have to be sidelined from risk of infection. If people are prevented from venting their feelings in one place, they could emerge at another.'

'The referee who wanted to sideline a player for verbal abuse had a sneaky mission to turn the game into a passionless nanny state Spectacle,' Paul said.

'The middle class keeps the alienated lower class feeling fearful and superfluous,' said Michelle. 'They are passive audiences intently consuming tickets to games, entertainment and food that De Bord (15) describes as a Spectacle, within capitalism.'

'Passivity is aimed for, contrasting with Marxist revolution.'

'Games are becoming tame, cool and calculated like snooker,' said Paul. 'Spectators will stay at home. It's the same in all sports. The nanny state goes too far.'

'The nanny state can prevent injuries. My new badminton racket has a warning sticker affixed. It says:

'Use of this racket can cause serious injury. Supervision by a coach is recommended.'

'They must be covering themselves against eye injury,' said Michelle.

'That notice gives me the creeps,' Paul said. 'I don't dispute that accidents occur from recklessness. It's questionable that using a badminton racket has significantly more danger than riding a bicycle, throwing a javelin, shooting an arrow, driving a car, or boiling an egg, but those don't have labelled warnings. Vulnerable people may not be deterred by warnings. Many people learn about dangers by trying new things. But the danger to a novice from a badminton racket is difficult to anticipate. There isn't much a player can do about it, other than aiming away from opponents. It doesn't need to be labelled as a danger. A person can fall on to the ground and hurt themselves, but shoes don't have safety instructions.'

'It's not necessary for most people,' Michelle said.

'Intelligent adults don't need a nanny.'

'Don't we need to protect the young and foolish?' Michelle asked him.

'Of course, but it is a question of degree,' he said. 'Without protection, we have survival of the fittest, in a Hobbesian state of nature, red in tooth and claw. Everyone wants protection from the worst dangers.'

'Hidden dangers are banned, for example drugs,' Michelle said.

'The overreach of the state can interfere, beyond providing protection,' Paul said. 'The stolen generation of indigenous children is an example. Australian governments, in a fit of cultural hegemony and moral certitude, encouraged by religion, removed children of whatever race from inadequate parents 'for their own good''.

'They have received an apology from a Prime Minister, as if the mistake was racism against 'blacks,' he said. 'White' children from inadequate homes were taken too. The nanny state could have provided practical help to parents struggling to raise their children. It would have been less divisive. We have too much faith that the nanny state will look after everyone. Australia's nanny state is pervasive and individualism is threatened.'

'The threat to individuals is removal of personal choice by state control,' Michelle said. 'It is coercive paternalism. It deliberately deters adults from doing what they want to do.'

'Regulation of food, alcohol, sugar and smoking are most visible.'

'The soviet experience went further, into totalitarianism. The nanny state can bring hellish living conditions and mind numbing jobs, as experienced by the Russian proletariat in the soviet era. The degradation then was atomism of society and superfluousness of individuals.'

'The nanny state reduces choice,' said Julia. 'Frank Chodorov, (1887–1966) pointed out that egalitarianism is not only doomed, but undesirable, because it threatens freedom.

'Freedom is essentially a condition of inequality, not equality. It recognises as a fact of nature the structural differences inherent in man - temperament, character, and capacity - and it respects those differences. We are not alike and no law can make us so.'

'Why don't you run for parliament, Dad,' Michelle said. 'That could be your manifesto.'

'Thanks Michelle. It's pretty close to what I believe,' Paul said. 'I'm not sure that voters want to be told they're all different and alone.'

'That's totalitarianism. Society is atomised. It's all around us today. There are people in despair because they have lost hope,' Julia said. 'You don't have to make them feel weird. What you can do is bring them together, so they won't be lonely and will trust people again.'

'That's populism,' Paul said. 'How can I pitch a manifesto with everyone alone and different?'

'People like to be different,' Julia said. 'A process of finding inequality can win support. People have to be consoled because there can never be equality of outcomes. It's a low entropy society, disorganised. You won't be able to recruit much energy. The individuals don't have much energy left.'

'When consolation has been overdone at school, workers may be traumatised and relegated to the bottom rung of the earnings ladder,' said Michelle. 'Teachers can show them how to get started. One-on-one coaching and lifelong learning can build resilience.'

'Totalitarianism can be countered by attention to individuals,' said Julia.

'The nanny state prefers to deal with people as an amorphous mass,' Paul said. 'It doesn't work.'

'Leaders are needed who can build up society from the bottom,' said Michelle.

'I could find out how to nominate for the senate,' Paul said.

'Would you join a party?'

'Absolutely not. I would run as an independent.'

'What would be your platform?'

Paul thought for a moment. 'Keep Out The Nanny State.'

'You could be the only senator who opposes the nanny state,' said Chance. 'Most of them fall over themselves aligning themselves with policies that kowtow to their electorates . . .'

'. . . whereas I will be trying to expose policies that do not serve the people,' said Paul. 'It could be lonely unpopular work. Perhaps the opposition would help me target nanny state policies. Hmm.'

'We should not be too critical of the nanny state,' said Michelle. 'Public welfare systems have delivered us clean water and sanitation, limited drink driving, required safer vehicles and regulated road safety. Besides providing universal health care, states have been responsible for child protection, educating the masses, supporting the homeless, electricity supply, product safety, food safety, environmental health, financial management, social services and vaccines. There are hundreds of regulations, standards and controls that work well. Sure, some people are inconvenienced, but stopping the nanny would throw out the baby with the bath water.'

'Our nanny state has helped particularly young people, without creating dependence,' said Chance.

'I'm not sure what over-reach there has been,' said Julia. 'What was wrong with having properly funded hospitals, council houses, student grants and free eye tests?'

'Nothing wrong,' Paul said. 'The nanny state has done much good. Nevertheless, nanny state over-protection is indisputable. There are too many people who expect the State to take care of them. It would be okay if it would last, but they will be jolted when the nanny leaves them. The Shell Oil Company had its own nanny state for employees and their families. It was found that when they retired and were denied nanny benefits, they died within two years. Employees who have made their own social arrangements can look forward to a long retirement. The nanny state kills people in the same way as Shell.'

'Having a nanny state doesn't shut off the benefits,' said Julia.

'No, but people get too run down to claim them,' said Michelle.

'Julia is right. People sometimes don't claim benefits due to learned helplessness,' Paul said. 'They give up trying.'

'Disaster relief by communities is an expectation of our nanny state,' said Michelle. 'You want to keep that don't you? When adversity strikes, businesses, property owners and workers expect help from the nanny state, especially when insurers become reluctant to provide coverage and pay claims. The nanny state has picked up the tab for temporary housing, evacuation and supplies. Compensation for disaster victims is widely supported, gets votes, is profitable and re-elects governments. Images of the state helping victims are powerful and the Spectacle goes from strength to strength.'

'Yes. But everybody is climbing on to the disaster bandwagon,' Paul said.

'You are saying that because you are sceptical about climate change,' said Michelle. 'What is the nanny state doing that you want to stop?

'The nanny state has soft conditions for its adherents, enabling undeserving individuals to prosper and grab opportunities otherwise not available, taking from others who are struggling for the same opportunities,' I said. 'Hard work, risk taking and tough independence go unrewarded. Perhaps a nanny state betrays the ethos of hard work and competition that sustained our ancestors. Australians like to be thought of as rugged outdoor types. Our nanny state contradicts that.'

'You seem to want a macho nanny state,' said Michelle. 'Is it fair to exclude worthy applicants, when they are wimpy?'

'There is a stream of applications for money to mitigate global climate change hardship. The nanny state wants to relieve catastrophic climate conditions but it is mobbed by voices misleading them about what to do.

'State intervention should go beyond selfish benefit to the individuals immediately affected. The beneficence can, like charitable works, be meant to serve higher purposes of a wider group.'

'The state has taken on the charitable activities of religious groups, such as provision of shelter, accommodation and education,' Julia said. 'The state has assumed a parental role like a nanny. There are various philosophies how to undertake the nanny role. Socialists generally are guided by altruistic intents, whereas Christians follow the teachings of the bible. Although Darwin did not propose survival of the fittest as a societal policy, this approach was adopted as an extension of the laissez faire economic policy. Conservative politics are sometimes the antithesis of the nanny state.

'In nanny state politics, the nanny occupies the high moral ground,' I said. 'Conservatives and many liberals oppose it. It isn't usual for the sides to share benefits.'

'Independent individualism is more deeply rooted in the human psyche than equality and collectivism,' Julia said.

'I have been unpleasantly aware of the nanny state taking away my liberties and reducing the quality of my life,' Paul said. 'This has been apparent on urban streets, where I have been hindered by unwanted traffic lights, traffic calming islands, roundabouts, pedestrian crossings, pedestrian crossing lights, unnecessary road signs, parking zones, parking meters, no-stopping zones and one-way systems. Officialdom in other spheres has grown a morass of websites and complex forms of correspondence claimed to benefit a majority, but they disadvantage me. I am benefitting others, at a higher cost to myself than is reasonable.

'The nanny state has taken over the middle ground from libertarian conservatives with the prosperous market economy on one side and the impoverished socialist welfare state on the other,' Michelle said. 'The nanny state lies between middle class wealth and lower class poverty. Our nanny state has adopted provisions from the socialist agenda: working conditions; fair pay; women's rights; control of prices; home ownership; public transport; health services; welfare; public housing; and so on.

'We have a totalitarian city to the extent that it is ruled by a would-be-dictator whose policies are centralised and arbitrary,' Paul said. 'Individuals are isolated, atomised, superfluous and unimportant. It will take concerted effort by leaders and the city government to create a vibrant city where all citizens feel valued. Unless the totalitarian stranglehold is broken, the nanny state will remain an insipid force for change.

Chapter 10 Campaigns

Paul had a small supporter group for his senate election campaign. They were in Canberra; he was in Brisbane and he met with them on Zoom. They discussed federal politics and issues for his campaign.

'Suburban living in Brisbane is framed and mirrored by the media, businesses and political parties,' he commenced. 'They maintain a layered Spectacle having images of warfare, disease, flood, drought, climate crisis, famine and cost of living threats. The parade of possibilities keeps the population in despair, overeating and paying for entertainments such as sport and diversions to distract them from their perceived shitty living and working conditions. They feel alienated but lack the impetus to join revolutionary movements and are withdrawn, superfluous and helpless.'

'Are these your main concerns, Paul?' asked a friend, Richard.

'I don't think I can get far with a populist approach. Populism is promoted by aspiring demagogues to exploit divisiveness in elections. The nanny state embraces the Spectacle and governments fund investment in renewable energy without considering obvious consequences such as electricity generation mayhem. I want to present my analysis of issues and it is likely to be perceived as coming from right field.'

'Perhaps you can attract a following with your views on smaller local issues, before the media take them over,' said Veronica on Zoom.

'Good idea,' Paul said. 'There are people who oppose the parties who will be interested in our local proposals. We need publicity material.'

'Our main opponents are public utilities who have promoted images of relieving Australians from possible consequences of climate change,' he said. 'The main thrust is for state electricity authorities to quit using fossil fuelled power stations and to reduce carbon combustion, as part of Net Zero planning to meet international obligations. Their reassurances had not alleviated some voters' concerns and they have contacted us asking my views on climate change.'

'The climate activists have stalled State authorities' approval of new coal mines for domestic and export supply,' said Richard. 'The royalty loss to state enterprises and unemployment is huge. Voters will be concerned that Australia is closing down.'

'Another consequence of climate change acceptance is resettlement in Australia of Pacific Islanders living on islands threatened by sea level rise. It is considered a responsibility of Australians whose emissions could have caused it.'

'The theoretical framing of bushfires as a consequence of climate change is causing nanny state expenditure on prevention,' Paul said. 'We can request more moderate responses, in line with historical experience.

'The nanny state's investments in solar panels, wind turbines, batteries, pumped storage schemes and electric vehicles should be carefully planned and budgeted. The authorities have been trying to rush expenditures and voters will want caution.

'The uptake by the public of new technologies is lethargic, requiring prodding by nanny state subsidies. Buyers have the appearance of taking on existential risk, serving the community better than their neighbours with their cautious inaction.'

'We need to question the shutting down of coal stations,' Paul said. 'The nanny state has loaded citizens down with many more obligations than benefits. It has seemed unfair to shut down power stations locally while allowing others abroad to keep generating with a higher standard of living. Nanny state profligacy is part of our Spectacle.'

'You are a have,' said Veronica. 'Have-nots want you to support them.'

'I want only to support unfortunates, not to have my wagon hitched to a nanny state trying to provide for people who are misled by liars,' Paul said.

Although the tide of public opinion was running against him, he would run for the Australian Senate. He had acquired citizenship when he arrived in Australia, as an immigrant.

He would run unendorsed by any party, nominated by 100 eligible electors as required. An incumbent candidate's self-nomination would be enough but he would door-knock and ask people to nominate him. He would be listed below the line as an ungrouped independent. His position as an independent had been made difficult by the parties, who had set the rules. His name, without a party identifier, would be listed at the end of the long ballot paper, where voters would be undecided and less likely to select an independent.

He canvassed in Brisbane to find support for a rational response to climate change, but the Spectacle was creating hysteria promoting images of climate crises to alarm audiences. There was no debate and people were at the mercy of the doomsayers and optimists. People wanted action and the nanny state was stepping up to provide it. People were in despair. They didn't trust the political leaders or the nanny state, but didn't know what else to do.

Andrea and Elaine came with him ringing door bells, until they became bored by the dull adult talk.

'I don't think you will get many votes,' said Elaine. 'Most people say they will vote for one of the parties.'

'My purpose is to let them know I am independent and have good ideas,' he said. 'They can decide whether to vote for me later.'

His independence came from his disdain for party politics. He couldn't accept conditions of party membership that would contradict his representation of constituents as individuals. In his view, a political party was a gang who commandeered the votes of members to exert pressure on outsiders. The causes they supported were not local and were intended to elect party leaders centrally

The nanny state was a front at which party members fought in a gang for election of a member. They were individuals who banded together for a cause. Paul didn't like to be opposing a gang and wanted to fight alone by force of testimony rather than by expensive advertising. The number of his supporters grew steadily and he had help with his door knocking campaign.

He had reservations about the nanny state in everyday living, education, employment, environment and recreation. Government actions seemed opaque and arbitrary. They pretended that everyone wanted something and to get agreement the leaders had to take over, as if that was the only solution.

His motto was: KEEP OUT THE NANNY STATE

There were many individual views and general disdain for governments' inability to do anything worthwhile. Action seemed to be stymied by self-absorbed talk. Paul wanted to represent people whose views did more than echo the developments promoted in the media.

Chapter 11 Nanny State Wanted

Paul's campaign to Keep Out the Nanny State clashed with the beliefs of voters who believed nanny state actions had delivered a healthier Australia, with longevity amongst the highest in the World.

'. . . we live in a safer, more civilised society, because of regulation around electricity and other trades, food safety, financial management, social services and infectious disease regulation to name just a few.'
I Moore, Why We Need the Nanny State, CityNews, 20/08/2015.

He found it difficult to oppose the nanny state because it was associated with popular causes and its failures were not exposed or talked about. There had been several large projects in the news that did not go ahead through lack of support or technical problems and this was attributed to the character of the projects rather than as failures of nanny state leadership. The nanny state was in the fortunate position of not being responsible for public investments that failed, but received accolades for projects that succeeded.

'There are many circumstances where a nanny state has helped Australians obtain justice and fairness in government,' he said. 'Most people want a nanny state to supply electricity, water, garbage collection, postal services, hospitals, prisons, schools, internet and employment. Public services are assigned to meeting these needs. But private services are taking over in some places, with improved delivery. Prisons, schools and public housing are being run by private companies.

'But doesn't the nanny state have to be run publicly?' asked Michelle.

'Public services have often been preferred,' he said. 'A theory was that private services would be more rapacious and would gouge indiscriminately. But that is a bias. Greed is encountered in both private and public companies.

'The nanny state is expected to employ local people and support the interests and prosperity of the community. The facts are that people can be treated better by private companies than they can be by state authorities.'

'Public expenditure by the nanny state was also wanted by Keynesians,' said Michelle. 'It was the rationale for kick-starting the economy during the great depression.'

'Keynes wanted public expenditure to lead investment,' Paul said.

'John Maynard Keynes, in 1915 joined the UK Treasury and advised the government for many years,' said Andrea consulting her phone. 'His idea was that that governments should play an active role in their countries' economies, instead of just letting the free market reign.'

'Private investors were expected to take a back seat,' said Paul. 'Keynes tried to impose unwanted systems throughout the state when those who would benefit were few. It was very annoying to be benefited as a lumpen prole. Individual sovereignty was disappearing, smothered and drowned in nanny state systems. They often meant well, but got carried away with hubris.'

'Recently, Smart Alek politicians have been second-guessing markets,' he said. 'They have invested public funds in businesses they know nothing about, creating an arch-nanny-state.'

'Your campaign is biased against the nanny state,' said Michelle. 'Your opponents will find it easy to refute your arguments with instances of nanny state benefit.'

'If the debate is balanced, it will have a good outcome,' Paul said.

Chapter 12 Nanny State Not Wanted

Paul's view was that the nanny state should stop coddling the public with projects that created dependence and should encourage independent projects.

The previous government had provided facilities, training and finance to entrepreneurs. A few developed viable businesses, but unable to sell their products and requiring assistance to rehabilitate the workers, most failed within 12 months. Often the owner lacked business acumen. The failures discredited the nanny state.

The nanny state had used to operate on a larger scale, with city-wide vocational training programmes for workers to obtain employment subsidised by large and medium size retailers. But these workers were reluctant to take lower earnings when the subsidy was removed. Their conditions of employment had been artificial and they did not learn as well as with critical supervision.

Left to their own devices, employers' training of workers was more satisfactory. The rundown in the numbers of apprenticeships was a result of other training available, possibly under nanny state schemes.

The nanny state had interfered with employment of school students by offering day release and apprenticeship schemes. Some were unsuccessful. They required further training to compensate for the harm done to their employment prospects. It was overreach.

Overreach on a larger scale included job seeker subsidies that did not result in employment. This was a negative experience for young people who wanted their work to earn at a sustainable market level.

The nanny had become involved in youth and employment programmes, trying to help youngsters to come of age and take their place in the adult world. This could be successful but too often was over-protective and students didn't discover opportunities to assert their likes and dislikes, gaining a tentative and timid hold on adulthood. When this happened, it could not be remedied by another employment programme, but rather the young person had to start again, by getting more education.

Many young people found their way more by accident than by design. If they discovered their own agency in obtaining work, no matter how humble, they could look for opportunities to improve their lot and assume responsibility for it. The nanny state had little to contribute except as a safety net for their tentative steps.

Paul felt that a 'nanny state' was seriously interfering with his family's lifestyle, the way that a bossy nanny would interfere with her employers' children. In almost every area the government was enticing people to spend, or to borrow for immediate consumption. There was little expectation that they should invest in their futures. His grandchildren were being lured into roles as 'also rans' without contributing to society, except by paying down the huge debt they had inherited from the nanny state.

Paul resisted changes to electricity supply, when the cost would increase, or the cost was not transparent. It was apparent that the expensive transition to renewable electricity was to be paid for by customers, by sleight of hand. Paul wanted to resist it.

His political group were opponents of nannification. They met in an informal group to discuss how to respond to the slurs, policies and lies of nanny state advocates. They did not seek donations. The group became influential and feared by the main parties for its criticism of their meddling.

By publicising the intrusive nature of 'nanny state' proposals, they discouraged governments from introducing legislation or regulation that would undermine the interests of individuals. They collected evidence of interventions which had been harmful, where the nanny state was interfering with the choices of ordinary people. They wanted to protect people from exploitation.

Chapter 13 Communism by Stealth

Communism is a sociopolitical, philosophical, and economic ideology within the socialist movement, whose goal is the creation of a socioeconomic order centered around common ownership. It was set back by the collapse of the Soviet system in Russia in 1991. There had been antipathy with the Western countries during the Cold War. When communism had failed in Soviet Russia, some adherents had concealed their leaning and become prime movers in growth of Australia's nanny states. The gradual insertion of socialist beliefs into capitalist economies had continued up to the present.

Governments in most countries tempered capitalism with increasing socialism. Nanny states were instrumental in the transformation. Capitalism and communism were in some ways complements. Communists wanted government control of goods and services whereas capitalists left it to buyer, sellers and markets to decide what could be sold and to negotiate prices. When demand exceeded supply, the price increased and the supplier profited from ownership of the business. When the business was owned by the state, it was state capitalism, with characteristics of free enterprise.

In free enterprise, the spur of competition and the zeal and zest of ownership aroused the productiveness and inventiveness of followers. A basic democracy ruled the process insofar as most of the articles to be produced and the services to be rendered, were determined by public demand rather than by governmental decree. Competition compelled the capitalist to exhaustive labour, and his products to ever-rising excellence (21p58).

Today capitalists, instead of receiving adulation for their philosophy, are beset by protests and revolts against their industrial mastery, price manipulation, business chicanery, and irresponsible wealth. It is these and other drawbacks, attributed to capitalism, that originate communism. Communists find faults in capitalism and want state control under state ownership, restricting what can be sold and setting prices to cover the cost of production, including state resources and labour, without profit. If there is a surplus, it is absorbed by the state. When demand exceeds supply, buyers must queue to be served. Workers can go on strike, unless the government intervenes and declares those services to be essential.

It is the ideal of state control that creates authoritarian nanny state conditions. A nanny state acts on behalf of a large group, closely approximating communism. Full-blown communism departs from free enterprise with additional levels of state control.

A long time ago, in Egypt under the Ptolemies (323 - 30B.C) the state owned the soil and managed agriculture. It was communism: the peasant was told what land to till, what crops to grow; his harvest was measured and registered by government scribes, was threshed on royal threshing floors, and was conveyed by a living chain of fellaheen into the granaries of the king. The government owned the mines and appropriated the ore. It nationalized the production and sale of oil, salt, papyrus, and textiles. All commerce was controlled and regulated by the state; most retail trade was in the hands of state agents selling state-produced goods. Banking was a government monopoly, but its operation might be delegated to private firms. Taxes were laid upon every person, industry, process, product, sale and legal document. (21p59). Conditions were stifling for former capitalist entrepreneurs but the system endured for 300 years.

Owners of the capitalist system may object to takeover by communism such as this, for various reasons. They would lose their control and income. Customers would have no say in prices. Workers could not choose employment and would be assigned to tasks by the communist government. They couldn't strike.

Controlling the communist Roman economy required employment of an army of bureaucrats, paid from increased taxation. The dictator Diocletian undertook extensive public works to employ the unemployed and food was distributed gratis, or at reduced prices, to the poor. In every large town the state became a powerful employer . . . standing head and shoulders above the private industrialists, who were in any case crushed by taxation. The socialism of Diocletian was a war economy, made possible by fear of foreign attack (21 p61). In Australia, during the pandemic in 2021, some people wanted a war economy, but socialism prevailed.

Socialism was also tried elsewhere. Socialism in China has a history of almost a century, from its origins in the 1890s to its gradual abandonment at the end of the twentieth century. On October 1, 1949, Chinese Communist leader Mao Zedong declared the creation of the People's Republic of China (PRC). The Communist Party of China (CCP) today claims to lead a socialist society, but since the 1980s this claim has gradually lost its plausibility.

China's contemporary economic system represents a form of capitalism rather than market socialism because: (1) financial markets exist which permit private share ownership; and (2) profits are retained by state enterprises.

China was unquestionably a socialist economy of the familiar and well-studied 'command economy' variant, even though it was more decentralized and more loosely planned than its Soviet progenitor. By 2020 China had completely discarded this type of socialism and was moving decisively to a market economy. China today is quite different both from the command economy of 40 years ago, and from the 'Wild West Capitalism' of 20 years ago. Throughout these enormous changes, China has always officially claimed to be socialist. The 'socialist' label lingers in China's credentials today, indicating the origin of their government.

Russia abandoned socialism with disintegration of the Soviet state in 1991, with restoration of individualistic motives to achieve greater productivity. Meanwhile capitalism has tried to limit individualistic acquisition by semi-socialistic legislation and the redistribution of wealth through the 'welfare state'.

Whereas Marx had predicted that the struggle between capitalism and socialism would end in the complete victory of socialism, year by year as the role of governments in Western economies has risen, the share of the private sector has declined. Capitalism retains the stimulus of private property, free enterprise, and competition, and produces a rich supply of goods; high taxation, falling heavily upon the upper classes, enables the government to provide for a self-limited population and unprecedented services in education, health, and recreation. In the East, the fear of capitalism has compelled socialism to widen freedom, and in the West, the fear of socialism has compelled capitalism to increase equality. (21 p66)

In all these experiments with socialism, what Paul was unable to accept was absolute rejection of the capitalist alternative and state control of aspects of life which could be under voluntary control. Calling a communist state a 'nanny state' was an insult belittling the maturity of the people, as if they required more protection than was available. The aspersion was false, as can be seen in countries with socialist leanings that have been able to develop with combinations of capitalist and socialist government.

Chapter 14 Learned Helplessness

Comparative government is about how populations are controlled. Besides differences in physical and environmental control, amounts of psychological control can have health consequences. Paul wanted to show that a 'nanny state' can adversely affect health.

Julia, Michelle, Andrea, Elaine and Chance had gathered to hear a science lesson Paul had suggested they would find interesting. When he announced it at home, Andrea called out loudly as usual:

'Science Lesson. Come all ye faithful.'

Paul hoped to interest them but was under no illusion that not everyone liked science. When they were seated he began to talk.

'Today I am going to tell you about learned helplessness. We live in a society in which many people are suffering from it. They have problems, are helpless and can't escape. I want you to find out how to avoid this.

'A nanny state can cause ill health especially when people are shepherded by someone they trust to invest time, effort and money, who assumes control and then puts them under stress. Gore's movie An Inconvenient Truth shepherded people unhealthily under stress to become climate activists. Their living was reduced. Seligman conducted an experiment that implied unhealthy people in aged care can be shown how to exert personal control and lead healthy lives.'

In 1991, Seligman studied the behaviour of rats. He observed the behaviour of rats in three cages, with 20 rats in each cage. Cage 1 had an ordinary wire floor but the floors of Cages 2 and 3 had electric shocks applied to the bottom randomly.

Groups of rats in all three cages had a few cancerous cells injected under their skin. Cage 1 was the control and received no shocks. Two of the groups, Cages 2 and 3, received electric shocks at random. The random shocks were supposed to be negative incidents that workers could learn how to suppress. Rats in Cage 2 could escape from the shocks by together pressing a switch, when they rushed to the end of the cage and with their bodies pressed on a bar, turned off the shock, for a time. Cage 3 could not escape from random shocks.

The effect of the electric shocks was to stress the animals, causing the cancer cells to grow. They checked for growth of the cancer cells to form tumours. Some rats died. Rats with tumours that had grown to more than 6mm were euthanized and recorded as 'died'. The experiment was continued until 50% of rats in the control cage had either died, or had been euthanized. The remaining 50% were still alive, having rejected infection by the injected tumour tissue. When the experiment ended, Cage 2 rats had the greatest number remaining.

Cage 3 had the fewest alive.

I switched on an overhead projector with a diagram and a table of results.

Cage 1	Cage 2	Cage 3
NO SHOCK	SHOCKED SWITCH	SHOCKED

RESULTS

CAGE	GROUP	REJECTED TUMOR %	DIED %
1	no shock (control)	50	50
2	switch off shock	70	30
3	shocked	27	73

Andrea raised an arm.

'Why did they give the rats electric shocks?'
'They wanted to find if different stresses would cause cancer.'
'Couldn't they have been less cruel?'
'Probably not, because it was the effect of the cruel stresses they wanted to measure.'
'In Cage 3, 73% of the rats died. Was that necessary?'
'Probably not. The experiment could not be done today. Since 1991, experimenters have been controlled by Animal Ethics Committees and when possible they have reduced cruel experiments on animals. For example, they could stop the experiment when 50% of Cage 3 survived.'
'Thanks, granddad.'

Paul described the experiment.

'Most surprising was that the rats who learned to switch off the shocks, rejected the tumours and lived much longer, on average, than the rats that had no shock at all.

'They used rats because it was wrong to give humans cancer and electric shocks.

'They used rats because humans wouldn't fit into the cages.'

'The conditions in the cages are like human working conditions with and without stress.

'Cage 1 had no stress and the occupants lived the medium time. Cage 3 stressed the occupants most and they succumbed to the infection. Cage 2 could reduce the stress and had a group purpose to switch off the current. They were healthiest, better than Cage 1, perhaps because they had a purpose.

'The key to the worker animals' health is their control over their environment. Seligman concluded when animals and people faced events they can't control — inescapable shocks, inescapable noises, unsolvable problems—they collapse, becoming passive, stupid or sad. Humans are said to become depressed (20).

'The animals with most control didn't entirely eliminate discomfort but lived longer with cancer. This suggests that more autonomous control in groups will result in a better health result.

'The experiment demonstrated 'learned helplessness', a psychological reaction. It is hypothesised that individuals will resist, taking control over unpleasant aspects of a nanny state environment and where the group can control their environment, they will perform better than others without nanny state control in an identical environment.

'Cage 2 conditions, despite electric shocks, had a switch creating an environment they could control. They turned on their hope circuits, activated by mastery and anticipation of control by unity of purpose. The rats in cages 1 and 3 suffered learned helplessness and most succumbed to the infection imposed equally on all of them. Some stress but not too much is better than no stress. Individuals having a say in their practical environment will be least stressed, healthiest and happiest.'

'What did the experiment show?' asked Elaine.

'It showed that if the animals were stressed, they would be less affected if they could actively control the stressor,' I said.

'What could be done?'

'If I was elected, I would protect people from stressful environments by showing them how to take group action to end stress.'

'That could be good,' said Elaine. 'Thanks granddad.'

'It also shows that animals can be badly affected if they are exposed to stresses they can do nothing to stop. Can you think of any action?'

'Yes,' said Elaine. 'I would like my teachers to stop talking when I have lost interest.'

'How would they know when?'

'When they had talked about 10 minutes. They could have another 10 minutes later on.'

'Good idea, Elaine. I can tell I have talked too much.'

'Thank you for the science lesson granddad.'

Chapter 15 Nanny Rhetoric Frame

When people are together and there is an announcement of a government action, the response is often negative, with someone saying:

'That has to be the nanny state.'

'Nanny State' is a pejorative term and there is no ameliorative usage of the term, when things have gone satisfactorily. The 'Nanny State' doesn't get credit.

Nanny state dissatisfaction arouses concern as a criticism of government. An Australian study recorded use of the term 'Nanny State' as a criticism in health delivery propaganda. News media complainants were self-interested and wanted government intervention to cease because it threatened their business and private interests.

News media, particularly News Corp, coverage of health issues demonstrably influenced public opinion, policy action and individual behaviour, by setting the agenda, selecting the sources, and framing issues, events and people. Industries such as tobacco tended to favour individual responsibility and cast doubt on scientific findings linking products to disease and death. Industries tended to favour individual responsibility framing of health 'choices' and 'lifestyles' putting the onus on the individual to act responsibly and resist temptation. They also diverted attention from industry responsibility and policy choices designed to make the environment in which people make these 'choices' more health-promoting.

New York City Mayor Bloomberg was shown in an advertisement, in which a matronly nanny told people not to drink sugary soda from super-sized cups. The Center for Consumer Freedom said the advertisement claimed paternalistic government policies had threatened free choice. It had invoked a nanny state.

This 'nanny state' slur, was a 'powerful framing device' that prompted people to think of the 'state treating adults like children', restricting choice, providing fun and shutting down intelligent debate. It also deflected attention from the drivers of ill health towards government overreach. They wanted protection of people suffering ill health from their own actions.

The term 'Nanny state' was portrayed as an assault on freedom and choice.

'Nanny state' is used in Australian news media, especially News Corp, to discredit the regulation of health-related issues. The most virulent opponents of governmental action, to protect our health, are companies that spend billions on promotion and lobbying to influence smoking, drinking and eating of junk foods. Selling of alcohol and tobacco is also promoted by rhetoric attacking government nanny state health policies.

Topics addressed as nanny state issues were: pokie machines; e-cigarettes, sugar tax, lockout laws, vaccination, racism, speed limits, pool fences, seatbelts, bike helmets, firearms restrictions, smoking, regulations on food and alcohol.

It is difficult to give examples illustrating nanny state overreach, because when the error is blatant, it is usually quickly fixed. Apologists for the nanny state are able to list many small matters where it has prompted regulation of food and health products. The evidence is often situations of over-reach which have since been rectified.

When the nanny state harms people, the regulatory authority would act quickly to amend the offending legislation. The task here was to identify possible infractions and suggest alternatives. An overall appraisal of the nanny state could declare certain regulation tropes as toxic.

A nanny state concern was of concern in 88 articles that mentioned the nanny state. (22). An agent was named as responsible in 49 government and 6 cited generic authorities. The nanny state was framed as an assault on freedom and choice which is an uninvited and unwanted invasion of our private lives. Framings suggested it was growing, out of control and a kind of madness. Other suggestions were that the nanny state treats us like stupid children and is akin to killjoy wowserism. Others said 'we' just don't like it; it's a bad look; we don't have a nanny state here; we are fighting the nanny state and beating it back.

. . .A national survey found 46% of respondents felt the government had a 'large' or 'very large' role in maintaining people's health and 80% 'agreed or strongly agreed' that sometimes the government needs to make laws that keep people from harming themselves, even though 90% endorsed personal responsibility.

Various perceptions of the government's role in preventing ill health were: as an investor in population health; a leader in promoting salutogenic behaviours; and a partner in supporting individual good health. In Australia, the government had free play in this space with large quantities of public money supposed to improve community health. (22)

Although many people believed the government was important in achieving public health, there were various criticisms of the nanny role.

The motives of those imposing nanny state controls included 'Orwellian', 'control freaks' and Green-linked 'activists'. News media-hosted nanny state debates were dominated by opponents of new public health initiatives.

Paul concluded from the study that the term 'nanny state' had various uses, not all of them pejorative. Health authorities jealously guard their freedom to pronounce policies and comments in the public political space, where news is extracted and criticised. The role of the 'nanny state' seemed to be regulation by State, Federal and local governments. He considered the political space of greater importance, where the negative effects of these policies were advised and ridiculed.

CHAPTER 16 NANNY TAKEOVER

'The electricity supplier changed us to time of day metering last year,' Paul told Michelle.

'Has it reduced your electricity costs?' Michelle replied.

'Only when we changed our usage from peak, to shoulder, or to off-peak.'

Paul had made an effort to use appliances off-peak, but it didn't explain why he had been charged $0.00 in recent months.

On 16 July, 15 August and 17 September, his home electricity supply from AGL, which had cost around $80 per month, was $0.00, $0.00 and $0.00. His account was $781.21 in credit.

He had heard on the news that the Queensland Government was applying $1,000 deductions to domestic electricity bills. He had heard several rationales, from hardship, to miscalculation, to Government largesse.

Paul was not unhappy to be receiving free electricity but wondered if there was some mistake. He couldn't see how getting free electricity would help transition to more expensive power. It must be a political expedient.

His interpretation was that the Nanny State had taken over electricity supply and chaos reigned. His concern was that money did not grow on trees and a day of reckoning would come.

He aired his concern with his campaign group, who were trying to get a perspective on electricity supply charges, in a meeting on Zoom. They wanted to know who was setting prices and what the future would hold.

'There has been constant change in prices for the last year or two and we want to have an overall perception of electricity charges. If we don't like them, Paul will take it up with AGL, his supplier.'

'The aim of our 'nanny state opposition' group is to have the government back away from those nanny state involvements which draw criticism. Electricity supply is one area of difficulty.'

'Do you imagine you can oppose the nanny staters?' asked Julia.

'Nanny state complainants are without leadership and have welcomed my initiative. Rather than broadly based dissatisfaction with the government, their involvement is usually a single issue.'

'I expect you will get more interest from ethnic groups.'

'Yes. A group representing impoverished people living throughout Australia has requested support. They could probably get a better hearing from the socialists.'

'Capitalist greed can certainly be a problem for them, but over-reach by the nanny state could be worse,' Paul said. 'In principle, a nanny state is benign, suppressing individual desires, but I detest overreach that diminishes personal responsibility, replacing it with morality and ethics. A nanny state can become a police state.'

'You're right,' said Julia. 'It was tried in the Soviet experiment but it failed. If the collectivism you speak of takes over, will it fail again?'

'Last time, instead of openness bringing reform, people lost confidence and the Soviet system crashed in 1991.'

'This time it will be different,' he said. 'Psychologists have said capitalism nurtures the id and removes its limits. Individuals can operate wantonly, especially when corporate interests remove boundaries. Optimistically, a nanny state that curbs instinct could liberate a harmonious public will.'

'A nanny state could protect us from the bad effects on individuals' rights of competition, parity and the public good.'

'Nanny state provision is costly to the public purse and does not always bring equality to needy people,' said Julia.

'The term 'nanny state' is used to malign collectivism,' Paul said. 'People regard it as over-protective, smothering individuality, fostering freeloading, growing like a cancer.'

'A nanny state can have benefits,' she said. 'Australia's nanny state has delivered personal welfare envied in other countries. People have had a say here and our nanny state provides things most people want.'

'A nanny state has to compete with individualism,' he said. 'I am an avid believer in individual interest, as the locomotive of volition. I am deeply suspicious of the motives of collectives of do-gooders.'

'Individualism and social inequality have been fostered by existentialism and utilitarianism, displacing religion. The nanny state is an antidote to personal risk and danger, usually costing loss of authority, obedience and effort. You are using the term nanny state pejoratively, but that is a minority and libertarian perspective. The classical liberal view is of government that provides services missing from the market, promoting economic growth. Public housing is an example. You are supposing the nanny state imposes unwanted goods and services. Sure, there may be some excess, but that is not the whole story.'

'Most people want to leave social policy to experts,' said Julia. 'The bureaucrats do what they like - which usually isn't what I like.'

'People want a charitable nanny state to let them off the hook of their Christian consciences,' Paul said. 'People don't want to give to beggars when the nanny state has responsibility for them.'

'Many people assume wrongly the nanny state knows best,' Julia said. 'Its role has grown insidiously.'

'It isn't a conspiracy,' he said. 'The nanny state is an appearance, together with capitalism, in its various manifestations, as the prime mover of Debord's Spectacle (15), providing goods and services to soothe lower class yearnings. The nanny state aids the capitalists by mediating the Spectacle.

'The subtlety of Debord's analysis of the Spectacle is he blames capitalism for the Spectacle and wants to oppose it to achieve worker emancipation,' Julia said. 'He adopts the Marxists belief in alienation of the lower class but instead of revolution overthrowing the middle class, they become passive consumers of the Spectacle.

'The context of the Spectacle is totalitarian control,' Julia said. 'It is associated with dictatorship, central control, persecution and one-party rule.'

'It is a political morass,' Paul said. 'Civil society is decaying, communities are declining and the nanny state is taking up the slack, making provision for collective care.'

'People have become disaffected and are too fearful to look after their own interests,' said Julia. 'In my court of law, people expect me to resolve matters they could easily resolve themselves, if they were less dependent. When asked for an opinion, or to make a commitment, they cringe.'

'Do they cringe in fear or is it deference to expertise?' he asked her.

'Both,' she said. 'They won't accept risk or responsibility. Many people want a nanny state to keep them healthy, find them jobs, feed them and provide them with housing. State provision of health and education has been popular. Provision of disability services and tertiary education has run into opposition. Outcomes of over-protection and free-loading are being countered by making individuals responsible for themselves.

'The nanny state's domain expands until it begins to take away individual freedom,' Paul said. 'If voters sense the nanny state is grabbing their rights, they will vote against it.'

During the discussion, we had cleared the table and loaded the dishwasher.

CHAPTER 17 NANNY OVERREACH

Michelle joined Julia and Paul in his garden. A mock orange hedge was in flower, filling the air with sweet musk.

'Let's go for a walk in the park,' Julia suggested. 'We can talk as we walk. Michelle can tell us her view of the nanny state.'

The discussion continued as we strolled. When we reached the park, we watched a family of tree creepers on a stand of eucalypts. They were medium-small, mostly brown birds with patterning on their underparts, looking for insects on the bark.

'In a park near here, there is a sign saying: 'Beware falling branches! How ridiculous!' Michelle said. 'The sign doesn't protect; it merely exculpates the park manager in case of accident. A park is supposed to have some natural hazards, it's part of the fun of going there. We need to preserve our natural instincts. I once saw a sign saying: 'Do not throw stones at this notice.' The precaution is over-protective and offensive, as is nanny state intrusion. It angers many people.'

'There are two sides to caring,' Paul said. 'Public care empowers authorities and arbitrary controls. When public care is relinquished, people have to accept individual responsibility. '

'Perhaps a sign saying 'Beware falling branches' is the antithesis of a nanny state,' said Julia 'It notifies people of personal responsibility. Where there are no signs, would the nanny state accept responsibility?'

'No,' he said. 'Some would blame the park manager for neglect. The sign merely prompts individual responsibility.'

'That is what the nanny state does best,' Julia said. 'It applies moral consciences to persuade us to keep the impulsive and hedonistic id inside us in check.'

'It is state care,' he said. "I don't like that sign because it invites atrophy of my personal responsibility.'

'What's the problem?' said Julia. 'It doesn't take anything from you?'

'By reading that sign I will be alerted and have my natural caution reduced,' Paul said. 'The message can't be undone.'

'Is it overreach, threatening the independent you?' asked Julia.

'Yes,' I said. 'It assumes I want to be cared for near trees. It's not for anyone to tell me to be careful. The other side of care is responsibility. It reminds me to accept responsibility.'

'People should not have their wits dulled by instructions,' she said. 'Parks are places where visitors go to be exposed to conditions as in nature. In my opinion, the sign is overreach, without sufficient benefit to justify intrusion.'

'Dad, you seem to have done a U-turn!' Michelle said. 'You used to praise the government for cautioning people against dangers. Now you are complaining when they remind you of your individual responsibility. What happened with you?'

'I have realised I am a unique individual and I shouldn't be required to behave like everyone else, without choice or self-regulation,' Paul said. 'I should be able to do what I want providing I do not intrude on others' rights. Freedom has a responsibility to respect others' rights.'

'The government tries to give too much advice or make too many laws about how people should live their lives, especially about eating, smoking, or drinking alcohol,' said Michelle. 'They even give advice on healthy eating.'

'What's wrong with that?'

'They don't have a monopoly on wisdom about what to eat,' she said. 'No-one does. They shouldn't pretend they do. They're trying to extend government influence and people don't need that.'

'It's too bad some people eat wrong foods.'

'They have a right to,' said Julia. 'They can find out the hard way.'

'Perhaps not as hard as being continually reminded of 'right' choices,' he said.

'Perhaps the nanny state should be limited to small doses,' Michelle said. 'The nanny can go off duty.'

'Over-reach' is finely balanced in the eye of the beholder,' said Julia. 'Public authorities who implement nanny actions need to do what is acceptable to a majority, not an easy task, even if they are helped by a survey. I would want them to refrain, unless they are sure that their action is for the public good. But other people may be different and we are bound to have cases of overreach.'

'Nanny state overreach can be hubris and meant well,' he said. 'Plenty of people have followed nanny state advice about installing solar panels and regretted it. The nanny state authorised installation of renewable energy supply technology before electricity costs were decided. The premise of nanny state action was that the new electricity supply arrangements would benefit most electricity users. This was incorrect because many electricity users had additional costs and there were complaints of government overreach.

'Perhaps the nanny state is out of its depth advising and subsidising solar panels. People could be out of pocket. A nanny doesn't supply toys for her children.'

Chapter 18 Is Our Nanny State Dumb?

A week later, at Sunday lunch, with Julia, Michelle and Chance, Paul dropped a small bombshell.

'. . .Australia is becoming the world's dumbest nation . . . (because of) the removal of personal responsibility and the increase in the number and scope of health and safety laws,' Tyler Brule, Monocle, 2015 (8)

The faces looked at him, disbelieving.

'Who is Tyler Brule?'

'He is a Canadian journalist and editorial director of a mens' magazine devoted to consumerism.'

'What would he know about us here?'

'He argued that Australian cities are over-sanitised and Australia is a nanny state,' Paul said. 'Whereas a nanny's role is protective and normally welcomed, there can be accusations of interference and overreach. Many of the laws have been implemented in the expectation that they will reduce violence, or improve health and safety. He accused Australia of having laws restricting freedom, ruining livelihoods and small businesses, turning the nation into a nanny state.'

'Dumb is a harsh judgement,' said Julia. 'Australia has good reasons to be a nanny state. We are spread out and we need a nanny to hold us together.

'The nanny has tended to bully us. The nanny state is intrusive, an affront to our personal rights unless we have given consent. There is something pernicious about nanny state intrusion. In inter-gender dealings, lack of consent can be rape.'

'Are you saying Nanny state dealing is covered up and hidden from view?' he asked.

'No,' said Julia. 'It may lack the consent of the people affected.'

'Government of a state can be by a 'nanny' who has to take care of unable, greedy, unruly and innocent people,' Paul said. 'The role takes responsibility for protecting vulnerable people from dangers, others' incompetence, foolishness, bullies, abusers, exploiters and more. They are cared for, not raped.'

'Some other countries have less intervention than Australia, or their intervention is received more positively,' he said. 'Perhaps our authorities overreach more often. Nanny state 'overreach' in Australia diminishes personal responsibility and undermines self-control. When an authority treats competent adults like children, they learn helplessness and become dependent on the state, losing ability to take care of themselves. The state can become over-protective and authoritarian, interfering in people's lives.

'The term 'nanny state' is used in Australia to derogate and lambaste new regulations affecting civil society, sports, business or education. Those who declare 'nanny state' are calling attention to their opposition to regulation. When there is disapproval, the government could be disadvantaged and use of 'nanny state' is not as a term of endearment.'

'People in other countries are curious about how Australia's 'nanny state' compares with their own. They want to know if living conditions in Australia are better or worse than in their own country. Perhaps they could use Australia's experience to modify public investment and individual rights.

''Nanny state' is not a lever governments can pull to implement policies,' Paul said. 'It is the sum of intersecting public welfare and individual rights.'

'Until the French Revolution, people did not expect there to be government looking after their interests,' said Julia. 'They had to take care of themselves. But Rousseau wanted liberty, equality and fraternity. He founded national government to pursue these beliefs, binding citizens together with a social contract.

'Rousseau required all people to act for the public good under state control. The Soviet experiment with communism prescribed state control of religion, health, education, employment, manufacturing, commerce and election of leaders. When people withdrew their support from the 'nanny', the Soviet state failed.'

'Perceptions of good government vary,' he said. 'The Gillard Australian government was hailed as successful because of the large number of new laws it passed while in office. To me, this was evidence of over-bureaucracy by a rampant nanny state. Parliament neglected other more important duties, such as debating and deciding issues.'

'Unless there are laws, the police can't control behaviour.'

'If troublemakers know what the standards of behaviour are and the punishments for transgression are known, they can control their behaviour. Fewer police are needed.'

'Some countries like Singapore are reputed to have many more regulations and restrictions on citizens' lives than other countries,' said Julia. 'In a recent survey in 30 European countries, Germany was found to be least restricted in regulation of alcohol, tobacco, food and vaping.'

'Perhaps Germans are least well off,' he said.

'No,' Julia said. 'Regulation is not needed when people choose wisely. A reason to be without those regulations is free choice. Governments have legislated to control thousands of products and situations unnecessarily.

'Conditions in Australia could require more government protection than in most countries because we have long distances between sparse populations in the interior,' she said. 'Populations have grown at compelled settlements with a predilection for governments espousing egalitarian values. Australians can now freely choose not to live in places where climate extremes prevail. Inheritance of a home at a warm location could deserve sympathy from the nanny state.'

'I agree that Australia has chosen to relieve its people of many hardships, with fairness,' Paul said. 'Both labour and liberal governments pay lip service to equality and invest in the public interest, such as infrastructure and social housing. More than in America, Australians have government provision for those who are unlucky or unfortunate, with disabilities, illness, victims of crime, prisoners, unemployment, or needing services such as electricity, water, hospitals, schools and internet at remote locations. Provision is also needed for the very young and the very old. Shortfalls in representation and provision for indigenous people are being considered for affirmative action.'

'Is that a type of nanny state provision?'

'Yes, but narrower and more focussed. Affirmative action is a set of policies and practices within a government or organization seeking to benefit marginalized groups.'

'Australians regard themselves as living in a lucky country,' said Julia. 'The nanny state in Australia attempts to reconcile provision at remote locations by egalitarian government. Inequalities of location, between city and outback, are difficult for private businesses to serve equally. Subsidised nanny state services, are often preferred, rather than internal migration.'

Michelle had been listening closely.

'Nanny state provision may not be a panacea, because it can diminish personal responsibility,' she said. 'The irony of nanny state hegemony is reduced self-care. For Australians, this could increase individual taxes and local collective action when summonsed.

'Australia's government was often criticised for overreach when new laws cut across private interests and across the prerogatives of the wealthy.'

'We're steeped in nanny state laws,' I said. 'We have mandatory bicycle helmet laws, gun control laws, prohibitions on alcohol in public places, plain packaging for cigarettes, pub and club lockout laws and permits for picnics on the beach. These are only a few. They are ridiculous. These matters used to be decided by voluntary individual control. A senate enquiry investigated laws and regulations that 'restrict personal choice for the individual's own good.' It's an oxymoron. Australia's criminal legislation has gone too far.'

'Our gun control laws are reasonable,' Michelle said. 'Other nations envy us.'

'It is an exception,' said Julia. 'A nanny state excessively controls, monitors, or interferes with people's private actions or behaviours that are deemed unhealthy or unsafe.'

'What do you think is state-like about a 'nanny state'?' I asked.

'The term probably echoes 'nation state', which is a body of related people in a country,' said Michelle. 'A nanny state has a nanny figure parodying a monarch. The government may be autocratic and resented by the people.'

'Utopians like George Orwell have satirized cradle-to-grave care by the state,' he said. 'Scandinavian welfare comes closest to that. Israel, Cuba and former Soviet countries have achieved some success, but opinions about this differ.'

'Some people want the state to supply everything, with little or no personal expense!' said Michelle. 'They dream of being securely employed under good conditions, without having to compete with others! To them, being without luxuries would not matter, because everyone would be without them. But equality has never been achieved.'

'In his book 1984, Orwell satirised a totalitarian hell, with state control of every aspect of life, including consorting, thinking and talking,' he said.

'During the Covid pandemic, various technologies were proposed to be mandated: quarantine, masking and vaccination,' said Michelle. 'There was a move towards mandatory vaccination but there was such a howl of protest, they dropped it.'

'Most interventions have been adopted democratically and objectors are usually a minority,' Paul said. 'Aboriginal people have had the state nanny doling out welfare payments, alcohol and housing.'

'Objection to nanny state provision is sometimes attributed to haves, capitalists, authoritarians or conservatives,' said Michelle. 'Nanny state supporters are labelled socialists and sometimes derided as have-nots and free-loaders.'

'Babying adults is self-defeating,' he said. 'The baby gets thrown out with the bath water. Provisions intended to keep streets safe for pedestrians, sometimes have the opposite effect. Zebra crossings and traffic calming obstacles encourage mindlessness on the streets. Children do not learn to cross the road safely. They step out into a zebrafied trap and are squashed.'

'Drivers should stop,' said Andrea, who had joined them.

'They should stop when someone wants to walk, but children sometimes dart out.'

'Poor people expect a nanny state to subsidise their rents, as if the market is incapable of charging them a fair price.' Paul said. 'They are like babies, fed by umbilical cord. They cling to benefits that others have had to work to achieve.'

'Electricity users, instead of using less power, expect the government to pay the increases,' said Michelle.

'Our nanny state sometimes helps with the cost of disabilities and this is just,' he said. 'When claimants get away with faking symptoms, others could have to pay for them. I had a student who claimed to have dyslexia and she was required to write her exams on dark purple paper with a black pen. I had to take it out into bright sunlight to mark it. I was ruining my own vision catering to her faked needs, when I realised her ruse was a rebellion. I refused to take part. When she was forced to comply, her performance was acceptable'.

'When a nanny state wants to discriminate positively, the validity of the claim and its provision have to be administered, at significant cost to the community,' said Michelle. 'The cost of the nanny state service can be excessive.

'When you encounter nanny state overreach, please call it, for the rest of us,' Paul said. 'However laws may protect only a few people some of the time. They don't work for all the people all the time. Australia is not the World's dumbest nation, is it? Conditions in Australia require us to have a busy nanny state.'

'Australia's regulations are appropriate to local conditions,' said Michelle. 'We're not dumb at all.'

'Whether Australia is over-governed is subjective and can depend on individual perspectives and beliefs about the role of government in society. Some people want a laissez faire government not to intervene, others want socialism with the state in control of everything. These are not dumb postures, but people's sincere beliefs about the role of governance in their society. Much effort and energy goes into reconciling the opposed political viewpoints.

Chapter 19 Utopia

'What type of society do Australians want? Do they want a utopia?' Michelle asked.

'What is a utopia?' Paul said turning to Andrea, who was engrossed in her mobile as usual.

She read: 'A utopia is an imaginary community or society that possesses highly desirable or near-perfect qualities for its members.'

'What would it be like living in a utopia?' Paul asked Elaine.

'Everyone could do what they liked.'

'If everyone did what they liked,' he said, 'we would soon degenerate into a dog eat dog world, a state of competition that would descend to the least common denominator of anarchy and chaos.'

'Get along with you. People are not that bad!' said Michelle.

'Many are stupid, selfish or easily led,' he said. 'That doesn't mean they need totalitarianism or a nanny state to overreach and control them. The goals of many are the Spectacle.

'The Spectacle (15) has media which obscure the lower class's alienation from capitalist systems of both production and consumption. The public news channels are unrelenting in diverting attention away to issues that worry us, such as climate change. The Spectacle is a mad grab to escape an unpleasant reality. Society is driven by existential fear to consume escapist media entertainment, to consult services that reassure, to buy protective products, to take anaesthetic drugs that dull the pain and to overeat nervously. The fear industry is huge, profitable and totalitarian in its effect.

'Unfortunately the purpose of the Spectacle is to profit from investments in media and entertainments. It doesn't have any interest in national security, the built environment, the national economy or even people's happiness. With the Spectacle leading the way, Australia is rudderless, without even a lookout to spot rocks. The situation is dire.

'Marshall McLuhan in Understanding Media (17) in 1964 proclaimed 'the medium is the message'', Paul said. 'People's television choices ruled the national interest in those days. Then Debord (15) in1967 dug deeper to uncover who profited from, invested in and controlled TV and other media. Debord parted company with the Marxists who desired revolution, accepting media would be capitalised, rather than wanting middle class control ended.'

'In the 21st century woke folk are angered by the abuse suffered by the lower class and they want revolutionary workers' councils to oversee improvement.'

'But we can make do without a revolution,' Debord said. "Change doesn't have to be bloody. Woke masses are not being denied Utopia by awareness of social inequalities such as racial injustice, sexism, and denial of LGBT rights. It's more like a conflict between alienated classes.'

'De Tocqueville argues that it's only natural for the masses to allow an aristocracy to take over.'

'In order for the revolutionary intellectual anarchy to disappear, the majority of civilians must exercise their reason. But the author himself recognizes that the power that directs the mass will always be aristocratic because, as he says repeatedly, it's impossible for all men to have the time and leisure necessary to occupy themselves with works of the mind.
De Tocqueville (9).

'Nietzsche in Thus Spake Zarathustra (1883) thought that society should be run by an aristocracy of guardians like in Plato's book: Republic. It was a role for which Voltaire wanted education of an elite, attacking the Catholic Church and advocating freedom of religion, freedom of expression, and separation of church and state.

'Perhaps privilege is the genesis of the nanny state - deference to elite reason,' said Julia. 'It used to be called noblesse oblige. We now want people to sacrifice themselves for the welfare of the community, for example by changing from cheap to expensive electricity. Care for others is romantic, but selfishness is more reliable.'

'The nanny-state is idealistic and romantic, but not everyone wants that,' Paul said. 'The nanny state delivers most benefit to those who grab opportunities and resources handed out by the government. Entrepreneurs persuade the government of new regulations that would win votes and line their pockets.'

'New state controls could be anathema to those adversely affected, but they can be outnumbered by beneficiaries.'

'Foucault (11) suggested that people *consent* to act in a certain way, not necessarily from free choice. Consent is manufactured in controlling mechanisms that produce norms, constitute interests and shape behaviour. This is how a nanny state operates, by consent.'

'People want a nanny state when they are fearful,' said Michelle. 'They scan the news continually for dangers.'

'The Spectacle(15) promotes the nanny state.' Paul said. 'Only approved dangers are allowed to make headlines. Mass media have taken upon themselves to censor controversial sources, using text bots to silence extreme opinion that would turn some of an audience away from established money earners.'

'The media interest is to create a news churn, slipping in subscriptions and sensational advertisements,' Julia said. 'Their touchstone for news coverage is to show provocative items, within bounds, that stimulate subscribers and generate earnings.'

'There is a role for censorship,' Paul said. 'Some dangers are difficult to avoid. It's necessary for the nanny state to divide roads, to protect people from erratic drivers approaching, but in most situations people need to retain the ability to evaluate risks for themselves and take precautions.'

'If we lose the right to full disclosure of risks associated with any treatment, we will lose motivation and move towards the socialist situation in which people can stop accepting responsibility for their actions. . .'

Dr Robert Malone, europeanconservative.com October 13, 2021

'I agree,' he said. 'By the time they reach adulthood, people should have taken responsibility for themselves many times. But, wherever I go, I am directed what to do and what to buy. They assume I want to be told, although most often I don't. I resent having to read signs and ponder the labyrinthine minds of bureaucratic sign posters, advertisers, spruikers and scamsters. No-one reads the terms and conditions that come with products and services. Suppliers dominate customers, a part of the Spectacle.

'I don't like it that the nanny state is taking us towards a narrow Disney world of thoughtless stereotyped behaviour and neglecting contemplation, exploration, discovery and choice. Parents and teachers know that without challenges, their children won't achieve much. When exposed to reality, humans will live long and meaningful lives.

'Bravo,' said Michelle.

He stopped and drank some wine.

'Not everyone would agree,' said Chance, who had been silent up to this point. 'There is a type of human who declines taking any responsibility for risks.'

'Homo patheticus,' Michelle said.

'But suppose you were struck in the head by a golf ball and reduced to a wheelchair, wouldn't you want the state to protect you, relieving your family from responsibility and looking after you forever?' Paul said.

Chance nodded. 'That's right. I would.'

'Wanting to relieve others is not the same as declining responsibility,' he said. 'A Nanny state can absolve the community from responsibility by shutting down activities in which injury can occur, but that goes against human nature. Humans have always taken risks. Our ancestors used to leap from tree to tree, risking injury and even death. If risk-taking is stopped, we could become like sloths, slow and vulnerable.'

'Sloths do okay,' Michelle said.

'How do you know that?' he asked.

'They don't go around causing trouble, do they?' she said.

'They could be caught in a cul-de-sac of evolution, without much intercourse.'

They laughed at that.

On the way back we saw a possum just out of reach up a huge blue gum tree.

'The loggers must have left that one,' Paul said.

'It could have grown since they came through about 100 years ago. It has been protected for the last 50 years.'

'The possum or the trees?'

'Both. The nanny state is not without successes.'

'It takes the risk out of living.'

'It is a matter of choice. The nanny state is a safety net.'

'Our future is stage-managed by The Spectacle and endorsed by the Nanny State. There is a process of democracy that elects leaders. The parties hark back to their traditions in framing the future. Their plans lack integration and are muddled, but no-one cares. The future is seized, project after project, by corporate barons for profit.

Chapter 20 Levelling

'All animals are equal' was written on the barn wall of Orwell's Animal Farm. In the seventeenth century a group of 'Levellers' in Cromwell's army begged him in vain to establish a communistic utopia in England. The socialist agitation subsided during the Restoration, but it rose again when the Industrial Revolution revealed the greed and brutality of early capitalism – child labor, woman labor, long hours, low wages and disease-breeding factories and slums. Karl Marx and Friedrich Engels embraced the movement in the Communist Manifesto of 1847.

Levelling can equalise performances of competitors by altering conditions of contest. In horse-racing it is called handicapping, producing a closer finish and more excitement than from even-handed gambling.

The future UK Prime Minister, Theresa May, argued that: 'Socialism is about levelling down. Conservatism is about levelling up. Socialists believe that, if everyone cannot have something, no one shall. Conservatives reject that.'

It was a philosophy that allowed ballet, theatre and professional sport to thrive. Levelling up focussed on elite sports and arts for people who could afford them.

Philosopher Guy Debord in The Society of the Spectacle (1967), recognised commercial opportunities for mass media audiences in athletics, rugby and other sports. Professional players needed different skills. There was an influx of non-elite players and levelling. Audiences appreciated a close game between traditional rivals more than display of elite skills. Audiences paid for tickets and the nanny channelled audience support into advertising, sponsorships and state politics.

Levelling made inroads in the performance arts too. Michelle and Paul went to see Swan Lake by the Brisbane ballet company. The Minister for Levelling had imposed regulations and dancers' abilities had been adjusted by the government's Chief Handicapper. Her aim was to equalise individual performers, by making ballet participation accessible to the whole population, by lottery, countering elitism. We were curious how performances would be changed.

Michelle and Paul sat together in the packed auditorium*[1].

'When I was young, I never had an opportunity to ballet dance,' Paul said.

'Isn't it wonderful that now ballet schools will take anyone,' said Michelle optimistically. 'All that is needed is good luck.'

'Ballet dancers have been an elite group,' he admitted. 'It will be interesting to see how levelling will affect the production.'

The handicapper had worked with the choreographer to dumb-down Swan Lake for first-time audiences of average cognitive ability. On a screen above the stage, a script of the story scrolled across. Because Michelle and Paul had been assessed to have large brains, they were required at the box office to place mental equalizers in their ears, tuned to a government transmitter. Their ear buds gave jarring chirps at regular intervals, to block critical thinking.

Suddenly Paul flinched.

'Ow! This equaliser is very annoying,' Paul said.

'It stops you overthinking,' Michelle said. 'It wouldn't be fair to understand more than others and have an advantage.'

A line of ballerinas stretched across the stage. They were almost all in step, but their leaps and twirls were ragged, with frequent rests, about the same as could be accomplished by an untrained sample of the public. Many had weights around their ankles, their figures were concealed by body padding and their faces hidden by masks.

'They deserve credit for trying,' said Michelle, as the audience clapped loyally.

'I'm not sure if they know what to do,' Paul said. 'They're not dancing in unison. They may not have practiced these routines.'

'It's good enough to convey the story,' said Michelle.

---

[1] *A fictional ballet scene like this was told by Kurt Vonnegut in his original short story: Harrison Bergeron. I am indebted to him and have adopted the unsurpassable novelty of his original staging.*

'Ballet should preserve traditional forms,' he said. 'It should celebrate physical beauty and fitness. This is grotesque.'

'I agree it's below traditional performance standards, but it expresses equality exquisitely.'

'It lacks the novelty of popular entertainment,' he said. 'It has the appeal of a school pantomime, in which the novelty is created by familiar characters in stereotyped roles. Artistic interpretation is minimal.'

Paul despaired that ballet was being destroyed as an entertainment. A sharp ping sounded in his ear and his thoughts fled.

Four dancers linked hands across each other for the cygnets' pas de quatre. Their heights and widths varied unevenly and they danced the piece with less than traditional mechanical precision.

'This demonstrates levelling nicely,' said Michelle.

In the two step, their rhythm was measured by the oboe, achieving a degree of synchrony in timing, but their footwork was clumsy and one slipped and fell over.

After that, the male and female principal dancers performed a pas de deux, but their athleticism was below average. When the male was required to lift the female, a stepladder was brought on to the stage for him to use. Her pirouettes were slow and the audience read a warning: SPINS CAN CAUSE INJURY. DO NOT ATTEMPT AT HOME WITHOUT SUPERVISION.

'Ballet is supposed to be uplifting, showing what dancers can accomplish through training,' Paul said. 'When not extraordinary, their attempts should be creditable.'

'Basketball players have been levelled to a standard height, to make reaching the basket equal,' Michelle said. 'The shortest can be lifted up by other members of their team, while tall players are on their knees.'

'It could improve the Spectacle,' he said. 'It will do away with the domination of the game by the tallest players.'

'We know that ballet was done differently in the past,' said Michelle. 'In those days the dancers led privileged lives. Ordinary people were without opportunities to be nimble and graceful.'

'People now expect success to be easy,' Paul said. There was a brief scream from his ear device, giving him an instant headache.

'They need to see excellence in order to excel and escape their mundane lives.'

'Attention! Remain in your seats!' said the announcer. 'A dangerous prisoner has escaped and is on the premises.'

Six months earlier, the corps' leading male dancer had defied the wearing of weights and had been sent for correction to the government's remedial institution. They had locked him in a cell, convicted of inequitable behaviour. Although he was irredeemably accomplished, he was sentenced to solitude so he could not inspire elite behaviour in others.

He must have escaped and now ran onto the stage, wearing tights, striding with pointy feet like a duck. He was tall and strong, wearing heavy ankle weights.

Without warning, he used secateurs to cut the straps attaching weights to his ankles.

He gestured to one of the ballerinas to partner him. She stepped forward and he cut her straps too, peeling off her padding, removing her hood, revealing stunning looks and a classic dancer's physique. They leapt up tentatively, then boldly.

Together they cavorted around the stage in longue jete', leaping higher and higher.

They were both in mid-air when an official walked on with a gun. Two shots rang out and the airborne dancers were felled mid-bound and lay motionless on the stage. Stage crew came on and dragged them off. They mopped up the blood and the ballet proceeded.

'We apologise for the incident,' said an announcer. 'We hope you are enjoying the performance.'

Paul was thinking he would like to see others rebel, but his ear bud bleated painfully. The device must have detected his aberrant thinking.

The possibility of another shriek in his ear made him cringe.

'Maybe the audience will benefit more with the performers levelled,' said Michelle.

'When pigs can fly,' he said. 'Equal performance is an end, not a beginning. Levelling has no place in ballet nor in modern dance.

Ballet depends for its attraction on excellence of technique. Making excellence disappear is a betrayal of individual fulfilment.'

'Shh,' said Michelle, interrupting. 'Ballet is going to be for everyone – no longer exclusive.'

'Too much has been destroyed,' Paul said. 'The Nazis burned books and degenerative artworks. Levelling at the ballet is a microcosm of a totalitarian state.'

'Oh phooey!' she said. 'Many people are enjoying tonight's performance.'

Michelle's optimism was endearing but differences between them were appearing with increasing frequency and threatening their harmony. He avoided confrontation but he felt vulnerable. They would continue to agree on most matters.

CHAPTER 21
SURVEILLANCE

Michelle and Paul discussed the ballet as they lined up to leave the theatre.

They discussed how outcomes could be made fairer.

'Opposition to negative discrimination may have gone too far,' Paul said. 'A popular Canadian psychologist has said there is excessive *intolerance* for inequality:

'America is besieged by 'postmodernists' who wish to build an economic system that will guarantee 'equal outcomes' for all individuals.' Jordan Peterson.

'He predicts disaster for a system attempting to make outcomes equal,' Paul said. 'Egalitarianism is the doctrine that all humans are equal in fundamental worth or moral status, opposing competition. People who are down-rated should be helped to improve. Equal opportunity is different from benefit of all and should not be allowed to drag down their betters.'

'We need to oppose the nanny state's sponsoring of immature adults, who are unable to solve problems by thinking and reasoning,' Michelle said.

'That would be affirmative action, which is discriminatory,' Paul said.

'Then not much can be done to level the playing field.'

'The nanny state concept has evolved in size and complexity,' he said. 'State care may have begun with protection at some time after voting began in Greece about 500BC, but devolution of power from kings, oligarchies, tyrants and early democratic rule, has taken a long time and remains an issue in politics today. The idea of a 'nanny state' that protects those in need, has emerged with the concept of a welfare state, commenced in the UK by Jeremy Bentham and the utilitarians.'

'The welfare state is one of the UK's most successful social reforms,' said Michelle. 'The utilitarians set up a series of rewards and punishments to civilize human behaviour. Regulation of health, penal and education systems spread to Australia. Bentham designed a prison at Port Arthur where prisoners were isolated from each other, removing their privacy, using surveillance to prevent them from learning from others' deviance.'

We poured outside and Michelle drove home, where she asked me in for coffee.

We continued to discuss levelling.

'The experiment with prisons was abandoned as inhumane,' Paul said. 'Nevertheless, in many places employees are still supervised like prisoners. As an office worker in Canada and London, I suffered under an excess of both physical and psychological surveillance. I quit engineering to escape from it.

'Foucault (10) described surveillance of workers during working hours, with social conditioning by behavioural and language control. De Bord associated surveillance with worker alienation within his Spectacle. Autocratic management practices were displaced by overreach of the nanny state.'

'Did the Spectacle emerge from utilitarianism?' Michelle asked.

'Yes, half a century later,' Paul said.

'Levelling would be more desirable for some qualities than others,' said Michelle. 'Levelling of wealth and property ownership would be very different to levelling of athletic performance abilities. There would be a lot of resistance, because it is cultural change.'

'Levelling could be our revolution, like China's,' Michelle said.

'It could be disastrous to devalue education,' he said. 'I am biased against levelling. It would take large change to create equality.'

'I'm not convinced the nanny state is really a threat,' said Michelle.

We paused as Michelle poured from a pot of fresh coffee. Chance came in and joined us.

'With a rampant nanny state, anything can happen,' Paul said. 'My research into competitive risk-taking indicates overreach can get badly out of control, with the nanny state promoting the Spectacle. Business and the nanny state are committed to profitable growth from private and public debt, borrowed from the elite. Nanny state intervention in sports is recent.'

'Support for paralympic sport is respected as a microcosm of a society wanting freedom from prejudice and corruption.' Michelle said. 'Sport and elite activities have critical audiences including people of lower ability who need to have their interest in participating represented, even if they cannot compete themselves.'

'A nanny cares for all her charges,' said Chance. 'Somehow the nanny state has to deal with all the people with disabilities.'

'There is a move to widen participation, with more equality of opportunity for disabled people. New rules are being proposed to allow participation by disabled individuals previously regarded as unqualified, who can now win in defined areas,' said Michelle.

'Elite athletes would quit rather than compete against disabled athletes,' Paul said. 'It's hard to imagine contests with competitors having mixed abilities.'

'Sport and performing have traditionally fostered competition,' said Michelle. 'Are you saying that couldn't be widened to include other athletic types?'

'It's possible,' he said. 'Winning isn't everything. There could be other ways of being involved in sport and performing that do not result in humiliation and elimination. There are people who resent others' physical ability who would prefer more sedentary, or alternative participation, in sports.'

'All elitism is under threat, not just in athletics,' said Michelle. 'The Spectacle of nanny state levelling in sport is motivated by the government's political agenda. The political parties are relating public social goals to relations between athletes. Everyone is supposed to be equal. The term *elitism* may be used to describe a situation in which power is concentrated in the hands of a few people. This may not be fair to the others. A select group of people is perceived as having intrinsic quality, high intellect, wealth, power, notability, special skills, or experience — they are more likely to be regarded as constructive to society as a whole and therefore deserving of more influence or authority.

'Is it wrong-headed to suppress talented people?' said Chance.

'Perhaps not, but levelling down the tall poppies could head off a change like Mao Zedong's Cultural Revolution,' Paul said. 'The elite would quickly lose their skills doing farm fieldwork. Such extreme levelling could reduce civil society.'

'I'm more interested in levelling up,' he said. 'I think I'll nominate for parliament.'

'Can individuals oppose levelling?' Michelle asked.

'They might not be able to,' he said.

'Many people will object to changes to the rules of sport,' said Michelle. 'Me for one.'

'Me too,' Paul said. 'We must oppose the nanny state before it's too late.'

'Also the Spectacle,' Michelle said, 'We must oppose it, if possible.'

'I think I'll nominate for the Senate,' he said. 'My ideas could get listened to there.'

'That would be great, Dad,' said Michelle. 'Many people will support your ideas.'

Paul hugged Michelle and Chance, said goodnight and left.

The talk of rules changes was worrying. The Spectacle was powerful. They could have to fight for their rights, an unpleasant prospect.

Chapter 22 Education

When he was teaching, Paul was frustrated for many years by the administration of the school where he worked. He had made several proposals to improve care for students, but they had been ignored. He was dissatisfied that his students could not progress as fast as they could be accepted by the universities.

'Our curriculum is out of date,' Paul said in the staff room.

'The curriculum requires students to experience all the main ideas when they are old enough to benefit,' the oldest teacher told him.

'How was the curriculum developed?' Paul asked.

'The difficulties of deciding a curriculum for schools was satirised in the story of The Sabre Tooth Curriculum,' the teacher said, 'at a meeting of teaching elders.'

''I am opposed to teaching science, technology, mathematics and English,' began an elder. 'We have always taught the catching of sabre-toothed tigers in pits, the killing of fish with clubs and the spearing of mastodons.'

''But there are no sabre-toothed tigers in the wild now, nor do our rivers teem with fish as they used to,' another elder said. 'Spearing of mastodons has been replaced by driving them over cliffs. The skills you want are no longer needed.''

''They could be needed again, when tiger numbers increase, when migration of fish resumes and when mastodons once again can be driven over cliffs,' replied the first elder. 'The old skills will always be needed, to guarantee our food and safety.''

''The old skills are also essential for students' general education,' said a third. 'When students learn to catch tigers in pits, they develop the bravery our people need to overcome the enemy who attack us at night. Clubbing fish requires concentration and precision needed in many occupations. Spearing mastodons requires athletic ability, to propel the spear long distances into a moving target. There is no substitute for this training. The old skills are still valuable and that is what we must teach.''

Now another elder, younger than the others, who had not spoken so far, addressed them. ''The problem is not so much what to teach about the future. It is what not to teach about the past. It is abundantly clear from 'The Sabre-Toothed Curriculum' that there are those who would teach the old skills to serve a dignified function of bravery, but they are redundant now. What is wanted are classrooms where skills are taught that solve society's immediate problems, enabling a majority of students, when they finish their courses, to be usefully employed or further educated to solve problems.'

'So the old Sabre-toothed curriculum was replaced by STEM subjects. Paul wanted education in state schools to focus more on developing academic skills but there was no way to change state schools except by central edict. Schools had begun as places where children were cared for while their parents went out to employment. Vocational studies now became student work.

Paul was frustrated that change was so slow.

'The only way you can get what you want is to start a school of your own,' said Nelson, a teacher colleague. 'You could teach what you want.'

'The curriculum would have to be approved by the Education Department.'

'Our curriculum wouldn't be so different. Our innovation would be the grouping of students by ability and promotion by performance, as we have discussed.'

Paul asked Nelson: 'Would you be interested in working in a school of our own?'

'Yes definitely,' he said, 'if it we could educate students for life, rather than wasting their time with all the nanny state curriculum bullshit we have here.'

Paul invited Nelson and several friends to join his group designing a new school. He wanted it to be a flagship for methods other schools could adopt.

They met weekly to prepare the documents required to submit to Queensland's non-state schools accreditation board. They supplied a checklist of responses for them to decide. They were helped by another new school which had recently opened. They borrowed ideas from their documentation.

They decided to call their school Constructivist College, giving it the name of their principle teaching philosophy. Constructivism is the theory that says learners construct knowledge rather than just passively take in information. It was developed by Vygotsky (1896 – 1934) a soviet psychologist. At the foundation of this theory is the belief that knowledge is not a copy of an objective reality but is rather the selecting and making sense of and recreating experiences. It was popular in Australia for teaching senior school students science, technology, English and Mathematics (STEM).

'How will our science lessons be different?' asked Nelson.

'They will be hands on, with students exploring uses of the equipment to answer the question posed. The new learning has to be related to what was previously known.'

Students would study in different classes for each subject and compete there for promotion. Non-performance would be corrected by repeating instruction and remediation of difficulties. Educational standards would be universalised, adopting requirements of universities and workplaces. A student could attain a high enough level in several subjects to enter university, while still attending remedial classes at school.

They planned for students to use computers to prepare them for technological workplace conditions. Both at school and at home, students would use artificial intelligence to solve problems, to create artistically and to analyse alternatives, such as optional purchases.

'The consolatory curriculum is a harmful nanny state intervention,' he told a meeting of their planning group.

'How do you mean?' Nelson replied.

'We have not been correcting students' work. Employers have difficulties with correcting workers who are millennials, because they often walk off the job,' he said. 'They come from classrooms where the consolatory curriculum has been applied and they are not used to getting criticised. Their teachers have rated answers to the sum $2 + 2 = 5$ as 'a reasonable attempt'. The student need to be shown how to correct this error. My granddaughter Andrea hasn't much self-confidence in maths. She hasn't learned to compete.'

'I agree,' said Nelson. 'Consolation is well meant but harmful. There is also talk about a universal wage. Could there really be equality? Workers would have to learn to meet work standards or move to another job.'

'Differential earnings have been the mainspring of workplace motivation,' Paul said. The nanny state in most schools requires students to be schooled in lockstep with age peers, regardless of different learning abilities. Schools are where children learn to conform socially and gain skills mainly by imitating teachers and peers. The classroom is a microcosm of society and students should learn to fail with dignity. They be learning to adopt a passenger role and being carried by their teacher.'

'Not everyone can be a cognitive star,' Nelson said. 'If they can achieve the cognitive skills being taught, everyone should have the opportunity to be rewarded like a star. We will have online delivery and individuation of instruction, with students able to progress much faster through course experiences.

'Social learning is also highly rewarded, for example, by appointment of student leaders. It encourages conformance. In most schools social learning between students is opposed by the nanny state, which discourages collaboration and group performance. Schools evaluate learning by individuals in isolation from others.'

When Paul spoke with parents, he asked for their support in having schools recognise students' varying abilities and needs. They wanted their children to have access to learning materials to the limit of their ability, and to mix with age peers of all physical sizes despite differences in abilities. In such a mixture, tolerance of exceptional students is wanted. It was a social solution. Students would make allowances for others less able or more able.

The Queensland Government's Non-State schools Accreditation Board website required them to supply a great deal of information about our new school proposal. Paul was surprised that they were considering 40 new schools. It seemed as though their application could take several years before it would be approved.

It was natural for governments to be careful about what education to permit their citizens' children to experience. The nanny state's approval of many aspects was needed for a school to commence educating and then continue year after year. They couldn't risk a new school graduating batches of misfits whose experience of the required subjects was deficient or flawed.

Their governing body had to be a company limited by guarantee and not ineligible for any reason. It had to be free to govern without unwanted external influence. The school would not be operated for profit and be able to make independent financial decisions. Paul knew several potential board members and discussed with them their plans, to develop their interest.

The school could apply for government funding and this would be determined by the Queensland Department of Education. It could be affected by conformance with the Department's standards of the school's board, facilities, staff and curriculum.

He began to have misgivings whether the innovative school they wanted would be approved. Starting a new school seemed to be an administrative challenge, having only indirect bearing on the learning experiences of pupils. There was protection of the students and their families but also nanny state over-reach in that there was over-protection from a wide range of circumstances that would caste the new school in a rigid system of values that could exclude innovative features that could benefit the students. Day to day operation of the school would have safeguards duplicating the cautionary framework establishing the school. His impression was that innovative planning was being deliberately disadvantaged by the nanny state bureaucrats.

To achieve accreditation, the school was required to uphold the standards of education at non-State schools, including prescribed syllabuses and maintaining public confidence. The nanny state had free rein to prevent innovation, especially if they did anything that the public could object to. The philosophy and operation of their school could be objected to by members of the public with limited experience and unwillingness to investigate or contemplate differences between schools. Board compliance would be regulated by exacting processes. They wanted the school to be innovative, whereas this seemed to be specifically prevented.

Their discussions with officers of the Department of Education indicated that they would oppose the innovations they wanted. Their plan for mixed-age classes and promotions by performance was unfamiliar and they objected. The officers had been teachers but had always taught in classes structured in the regular Queensland nanny state way. If they endorsed change, their jobs could be on the line. The old sabre-toothed curriculum was all they could teach.

Chapter 23 Communal Living

Paul wanted to move into a community with good friends. He visited several to see what commune living would be like. The lifestyles seemed intense and the sharing was spoiled for him by too many regulations. He wanted an urban commune where he could go out to work and then recreate in good company, rather than spending a lot of time together growing things and attending meetings.

He preferred to start a new commune where he would have a say in approving the regulations, rather than moving into one previously established, where he might have differences with the rationale and have to compromise. He met several people who could join him in an investment. When he had enough funds promised, he proposed a building plan, a design for facilities and a location where the planning authority was reputed to allow innovation.

Anton was a friend who wanted to join them. He knew him from sailing, where they had shared a yacht. He had lived aboard but was now looking for a berth ashore in a commune and they looked forward to living together with kindred souls.

So far, so good.

He heard of a wealthy family who owned several acres of land and wanted to build 5 substantial houses on the site - one for each family (grandparents, parents, kids and their off-spring) as a private holiday resort. They got knocked back and their eventual design was for 3 homes, one much larger than the other two and with common areas.

Paul met with City Council planning officers. They pointed out the difficulties of commune living. The disadvantages they said were that there had to be rules, or people would argue and fight, or refuse to do work a certain way, or wouldn't share money. People don't agree sometimes on who will make the rules, or how to interpret them, or how to enforce them. They conjured up images of `70s flower power and mung-bean-eating hippies. Modern-day communes – or intentional communities, as most are now known – are thriving, they said.

He wanted an intentional community, because there is less social isolation when people bond. Residents typically share common spaces, allowing for regular social interaction and group activities. This improves a sense of belonging and purpose.

He had visited an intentional commune in the country. Residents had separate houses around a dining hall. Residents had responsibilities of growing food or doing maintenance. The location was too far from the city and it didn't have the access he wanted to urban employment.

They found a 5 hectare building block not far from the city. The land was gently sloping with gum trees and enough space for 10 home sites a short walk from a single storey hub building, large enough for easy access to a kitchen, dining room and recreation hall. They expected to use these hub facilities for everyday living, although they could prepare food and eat separately if necessary. Sharing preparation of food would ease the tedium.

The planning regulations had never had ten houses on one lot of land around a central services hub. Local authorities were used to approving dwellings that were little boxes made of ticky-tacky and they all looked just the same. It was wrong that urban design was under the control of planners unwilling to allow diversity and experimentation.

Dual occupancy allowed 2 homes to be built on one lot, either attached or detached. A multiple dwelling could involve three or more residential dwellings, attached or detached. These could be apartments, flats, units, townhouses, row housing or built to rent. They could not be rooming accommodation, dual occupancy, duplex, granny flat, residential care facility or retirement facility. But each dwelling must include food preparation facilities, a bath or shower, a toilet and wash basin and clothes washing facilities. This would defeat the sociality and economy of the hub they proposed.

Multiple dwellings and families on one property could not be a solution, because if they're intended to be occupied by strangers, only two homes are permitted and there was a maximum time limit a person could stay there (2 days).

It may be possible to establish a caravan park with an ablution block adjacent to an owner's house. Indeed, some people are attracted to caravan parks by the sociality and economy. But the small size of the caravans and the impermanence of tenancy could be off-putting. Indeed the caravan park would have a licenced owner and permanent occupation by tenants would not be possible. It would not suit their needs.

They were getting desperate when they heard about community title. A community title in NSW relates to properties with at least two lots that share a common area, such as a driveway, pool, park or recreational land. It usually refers to large estates which could include several residential lots as well as common area for use of its 'members'. Community halls and spaces and pools are also common. It's like strata but with a personal title and also common areas where all owners have a *use entitlement* to that common area. Community Title scheme members would belong to a Community Association.

A central hub built on a site shared by say 10 adjacent owners could have planning difficulties. Community title may not allow a common area to be used as a communal kitchen, laundry or day-care centre. Joint ownership of the hub could be possible but linking it with all the houses could be difficult and an owner would be unable sell his share in the hub with his house.

By this time they were fixed on what they wanted and were not interested in starting a different plan.

From the point of view of the planning authority, regulations that would allow residents to share a kitchen and laundry would be resisted by equipment suppliers. This was not a legitimate concern but planners and builders work hand in glove. Sharing of pools is allowed, also cars, garden equipment and playgrounds, so why not kitchens and toilets?

These guidelines were so far from what they wanted, it seemed hopeless.

The planners didn't offer any hope of getting approval for dense housing around a social hub. Paul imagined the Council wanted to maximize ratable value and would demand the development blended in, maintaining appearance standards of the locality.

These nanny state obstacles were non-negotiable. Paul met with a local councillor who refused to challenge the planning department's control. There was nothing he could do but keep talking to the planners and wait.

The local authority's unwillingness to provide the living arrangements they wanted made the approval process for community title dwellings into a nanny state from hell.

When he was elected to the Senate, Paul's area of interest was nanny state over-reach and he used their commune planning experience to illustrate the planning hegemony they were up against.

CHAPTER 24 AUSTRALIAN NANNY

Paul was at a meeting, planning to nominate as a candidate for the Senate in the coming election.

'I will need signatures from 100 supporters and a deposit of $2000,' he said. 'I can get the signatures when I am door-knocking. I will afford the deposit myself.'

'What policies will you support if elected?' asked a team member.

'I approve of many government policies, such as free childcare. But there are several I will fight against, for example I oppose vision testing of elderly drivers.'

'Don't we need to keep dangerous drivers off the road?' a young man said.

'Certainly,' he said. 'They only check people who are over 75. That's not fair. They should test the vision and hearing of everyone before licencing them. By testing only old people, they are being ageist.'

That seemed to be accepted. He was getting some support.

'The State has done a lot to make life safer and more liveable,' a woman said. '20 years ago, life expectancy for men was 78 years and now it is 83.'

'I accept some state nannying is good but state control is expanding and taking away our rights,' Paul said. 'This was apparent during the Covid epidemic, when the restrictions on gatherings were protested. Some provisions for health, education and safety also threaten our freedom.'

'Is Australia a nanny state?' someone asked.

It was often-asked, with no simple answer.

'Is the government on the front or back foot with benefits and regulations?' asked a person wearing a hoodie. It was cold. Paul would not be drawn into partisan argument.

'The political left would be proud of social reforms made on the front foot, whereas on the right they would be on the back foot grumbling about the freedoms they had lost. I will mostly oppose social reforms that would be harmful.

'My political beliefs are for egalitarian conditions with equality of opportunity. I am less concerned about equal outcomes, because they are difficult to decide. Marx's idea was to redress class inequality: 'From everyone according to his faculties, to everyone according to his needs'. Since collapse of the Soviet State in 1991, collectivism has been unpopular.'

'The Chinese have done well,' another team member said.

'Layers of non-contributing people seized totalitarian power in Russia and China. In China, Mao Tse Tung implemented a cultural revolution with the middle class enlisted to work in the fields. Millions died from starvation.

'What answer has capitalism given us?' asked a young man wearing a flat hat.

'Nowhere on Earth has a community guaranteed incomes able to be earned without responsibility. The state farm people had no authority, nor any responsibility, to do their work. They allowed the food they had grown to be taken away. Capitalism gives workers responsibility for their production and brings them benefit from their work.

'In Western countries, the state is regarded as a 'nanny' that takes responsibility for all citizens, similar to a nanny's care for her children. Those like me who put down the nanny state, complain of over-reach taking care of those who could take care of themselves.

'The nanny state in Australia funds public safety provisions, where individuals in other countries may be expected to insure themselves, or take on risk. For example, Australian roadworks have safety officers controlling traffic, whereas in some other countries people can be injured by falling into holes in the road. Aged care in Australia is more comprehensive and longevity has increased. State intervention in keeping premature babies alive is extensive and vaccination programmes have been developed to control epidemic disease. Australians are protected by their nanny state, but sometimes it goes too far.

'During Covid, some people declined vaccination because preventative health treatments could endanger those treated. A nanny state may mandate compulsory treatment when unvaccinated people would act as vectors, resulting in libertarian protests and invocation of individual rights. A nanny state is supposed to protect vulnerable people at risk, not to threaten and control the unafflicted. For example, during Covid some governments closed schools, whereas other governments did not.

'Australia's nanny state takes care of the poor and many who could afford to pay for their treatment. When there is overreach and the state pays for services that the patient could have afforded, it is rationalised as generosity befitting a kind response to a group of unfortunates. Overall, Australia's healthcare system aims to provide universal access to high-quality healthcare while also allowing individuals to choose between public and private services based on their preferences and needs.

State provision of housing and health services is popular with people who suffer mishaps or declining health and are unable to provide for themselves. Like universal education, in Australia every citizen is entitled to receive high quality medical services, absolutely free of personal expense. Users pay for dental treatments, except for children.

'In the UK, the National Health Service has been an icon of democracy, a source of national pride. It has relieved low income families of the burden of treatment of illnesses and disabilities. Private health treatment is an alternative, with reduced waiting times and prestigious doctors who treat a few wealthy people.

'Australians can subscribe to private medical insurance relieving patients from medical treatment that could be prohibitively expensive. However, it is unlikely to be afforded without a good income. The public hospital system treats the poor and those without insurance. There may be some stigma in using the public health system but the preference is for a system of voluntary payment rather than compulsion.

'Maternity leave is provided through the government's Paid Parental Leave (PPL) scheme. Under this scheme, eligible working parents, including birth mothers, adoptive parents, and same-sex couples, can receive up to 18 weeks of paid leave at the national minimum wage. Additionally, many employers offer maternity-leave benefits. Australia also provides paternity-leave through the government's Dad and Partner Pay scheme. Both maternity and paternity leave in Australia are generally accompanied by job protection, meaning that employees after their leave are entitled to return to their previous position or a comparable role.

'Childcare is means-tested and can be fully paid.

'Full-time employees in Australia, are entitled to a minimum of four weeks (20 days) of paid annual leave per year, based on ordinary hours of work.

'Australians are protected by the nanny state. They are dismayed by US gun laws. Can it be that the American Civil War engendered such hatred in the population that they still imagine fighting neighbours with guns? With apology to indigenous people for belittling their fight for survival, Australian ancestry does not include large scale armed civil conflict. Australians generally regard their American neighbours with fond tolerance. Possession of weaponry could prevent mutualism developing. Occasions that would benefit from gun ownership seem few.

'Armed with self-righteousness, nanny state advocates in Australia have enacted a welter of regulations for everything from bike helmets to nappy pins. While these may protect some of the people some of the time, life with so much regulation can be unbearable.'

'Safe nappy pins are important.'

'The point is, the regulations are that the types of products for sale must be safe. When we drove across the State border, there was a large sign by the road;

You are now leaving the Nanny State.

Absolutely NO restrictions for the next 50 miles

NO cameras
NO speed limits
NO road markings
NO lighting
NO crash barriers

NO warnings
NO emergency help
NO hard shoulder
NO road maintenance

HAVE A SAFE JOURNEY

'It is rather chilling to realise how much we take for granted and how much we could do without,' Paul said.

'The nanny state in Australia protects people from hardship, arguably with some over-reach and over-protection,' said Julia. 'The consequences are there is more personal security but less self-reliance than in some countries.'

Chapter 25 Australian Privilege

When people learned of Paul's preoccupation with the nanny state, they sometimes assumed he was well-off and expressing disregard for people less fortunate than himself. They assumed that he could afford any services he needed and would deny them to others less fortunate. He was not nearly that selfish. His education had been privileged, he had worked hard and saved enough to be comfortably off. His circumstances were an enviable position in the class war, in which he found himself on the opposite side from people with a levelling intent.

Ayn Rand believed that selfishness is a virtue. In the introduction to her collection of essays on ethical philosophy, The Virtue of Selfishness, Rand writes that the 'exact meaning' of selfishness is 'concern with one's own interests'.

Despite Rand's recommendation, he found it hard to believe that he was a good person because he was selfish, but it was convenient to accept it, until he heard some other account.

He was perceived to be comfortably off despite living modestly. He opposed state benefits that others regarded as their rights. They received a trickle of state benefits that relieved the tedium of their constrained incomes. It gave them hope of justice, of a bonanza when their oppression would be lifted

He volunteered to help people in need who had been unsuccessful in seeking nanny state benefits. If he was elected, his work in the Senate would be concerned with refugees and asylum seekers. Each case was different and investigating the government position took a lot of time with the overall aim of controlling immigration. It was difficult to deal with residency applications fairly without stimulating boat arrivals. But most of his time would be taken advising constituents petitioning for favourable treatment of immigrants by the nanny state. The nanny state maintained an inhumane face to deter applicants.

'My policy is to oppose the nanny state,' he told a campaign meeting. 'If I am elected I will vote against legislation that would reduce constituents' freedom to choose what they want for themselves. Their lives have too many regulations and require too many permissions. The nanny state imposes on them what they could choose for themselves. Too many people have something imposed on them that they don't want.'

The anti-elite perspective was valid, because Australia's wealth was concentrated, with the majority held by a few people. When the nanny state granted benefits to low earners, high earners usually paid. The wealthy opposed the benefits distributed and either didn't need them, or regarded the cost as exorbitant. Their reaction was to bad mouth the 'nanny state'.

Their enmity made Paul sad, for he did not wish to reduce state benefits and if a person was deserving, he wanted them to be treated fairly. His good fortune was somewhat embarrassing but he could not contemplate giving away his inheritance: that would have abrogated his father's wishes. His father had acquired his modest fortune through hard work and the least Paul could do was to honour him by using it cautiously.

Chapter 26 Nanny State Dependable?

'The government 'nanny' is required to care for the public, but it is a large tasks and the government may not take care of everyone as well as it should,' Paul said, speaking in a forum to West End voters as a candidate in the State Election. 'Voters want to have their wants represented and that is what I plan to do if you elect me.'

'The nanny state is the face of public supply of essential services, that are difficult to purchase privately and crucially are expected to be reliable at all times. Government authority has strayed into provinces where there is currently great uncertainty. Established services such as electricity and health, may not be available.

'I will contend that if it is relaxed, the watchful eye of a nanny state may be unable to secure essential services like electricity and water for its citizenry, because climate change has made it difficult to anticipate new technological situations.

'The 'Spectacle' of renewable energy holds the masses' attention, in ignorant bliss, for power and profit. The Spectacles have both truth and falsity, catering for easy thinking, laziness and irresponsibility, a trap for the many. The alienated proletariat passively watches entertainments, which absorb their incomes and profit the bourgeoisie.'

'They are a harmful mutualism,' called out a member of the audience. 'The bourgeoisie and proletariat don't need each other.'

'Thanks for that comment,' he said. 'I won't comment except to say that I regret the division of the people into classes. I try to treat everyone equally.

'I do not profit from the Spectacle,' Paul said. 'De Bord portrayed the proletariat as inactive because they are stuffed with food and drink they have purchased.'

'We want you to lead us,' another said.

'I can help you with that,' Paul said. 'People want someone in charge they can trust, who will seem to succeed and who entertains them with his or her performance in office, convincing them that current conditions are being continued. A leader's performance is bespoken rather than analysed. Leaders usually lack qualifications to lead technological decision making and may be seduced to assume responsibility. My aim is to replace token leaders with responsible caring ones, such as myself. I have some proposals.

'Flooding of the Brisbane River is an example of civic neglect I want ended.

'Buildings have been constructed observing flood height restrictions, safety, fire alarms and fire escapes. But more is needed.

'The agent said my apartment, built in 1996, could never be flooded by the river, because a large dam had been built at Wivenhoe on the Brisbane River in 1985. He said the dam would have prevented water flooding the building site in 1974. The apartment building had been built at the 'defined flood level', meaning that the river could never come up higher.

'But the garages in the basement did flood in 2011. I proposed at a body corporate meeting that we agree an early warning system, with an evacuation plan and steps residents could take to minimise damage and losses. They listened politely and ignored my proposals. They were suspicious of each other with community taking second place to independent action.

'The body corporate manager exhaustively nannied the residents to remedy community problems but precautions against flooding were not implemented.

'In 2022, the unthinkable happened again and a flood filled the garage. Contents insurance compensated us for items lost. At some other flooded buildings, the nanny state admitted liability for homes completely immersed, with buyback of some properties. I couldn't get building insurance to cover my structure and fixtures. If my apartment was flooded, I would have to pay for it to be rebuilt.

'I feel that the government was remiss in approving our apartment building by the river, without recourse if the water came to that height. I had heard that when a local council had raised the defined flood level and disallowed a building plan they had previously approved, the builder sought and obtained hefty compensation for loss of building approval. It was the kind of nonsense that occurs when governments became confused with social concerns.

"I expect that there are some of you who have had similar experiences and live in flood-prone homes.

'The government's excuse for misleading home buyers with promises of flood mitigation is that people want the government to regulate approval of buildings so that developers can build homes and the Council can collect rates. It was a nanny state response that pretended nothing could be done to keep the flood prone homes dry and they did not resume the river dredging that had prevented major flooding during the 20th century until 1996, with the 1974 flood exceptional.

'My other gripe with the City Council was that the likelihood of further flooding of our home was increasing because they were allowing 55 bridge support piers to be built in the river channel, blocking sediment and flotsam from getting away. They had allowed the river channel to obstruct more flood water. Increase in obstacles to flow of floodwater included sediment built up after river dredging ended. Floods at our apartments would be significantly higher than earlier.

'The river authority claimed that obstruction was negligible. Of course they would say that, because it contradicted their flood mitigation efforts in building dams.

'I complained to the City Council that the government had misled me and I should be compensated. They denied liability, hiding behind the fine print in the Planning Act.

''We can't be responsible for every eventuality,' they said.' 'When you couldn't get building insurance, you must have realised your vulnerability.'

'The Council has accepted liability for some flooded homes and bought them back. Why not ours?'

There was applause from the forum audience.

'They say there are too many applicants and funds are limited. The nanny state's intervention was half-hearted. The possibility of being flooded, the government's lackadaisical attitude to flood mitigation by dredging, the unavailability of insurance, the uncertain availability of compensation if we are flooded, all cast a shadow over our home. The nanny state has not been as bounteous as it could be.

'Another instance of lax government is civic neglect in leadership of response to climate change. For example, it is widely reported that there is no possibility of the Net Zero climate campaign abandoning its failing opposition to fossil fuels, but no other action is being considered. It seems to be enough for the audience of 'couch potatoes'. Without electricity supply from other sources, the government has continued to hoist like a sail a proposal for nuclear power and green hydrogen, as if it could pull the nation forward out sail out of difficulty. It is a false dream that exploits energy users.

'The post-modern theories of philosophers De Bord and Baudrillard warn us against following The Spectacle. We are more likely to evade reality, concerning ourselves instead with things that don't matter at all, such as bovine emissions of greenhouse gases. Questions about the causes of climate change need to be asked, questions it is not now polite to ask.

'The post modern approaches invite us to dismantle traditional, boring and unfruitful beliefs about climate change and adopt new views that are more realistic and have potential for happiness.'

'Our future seems caste in the prognostications of invisible climate gurus,' I said. 'If I am elected, I will demand the nanny-state presents more objective information about prevention of flooding.'

The forum finished and Paul was surrounded by well-wishers. Some asked to join the group or to share experiences they had suffered by the indifference of the nanny state.

Chapter 27 Net Zero Strategies

After our community forum, a writer for local television interviewed me. I knew him from other meetings. He came to my home and set up a microphone and camera.

'What do you hope to achieve by election to the Senate?' he asked me.

'I want to alter the parties' blinkered strategies to aim for practical goals that are more realistic.'

'What is blinkering the parties?' he asked.

'They imagine they have to do something about the climate, without a definite idea of what to do. They have borrowed some proposals from a conference held in Paris.'

'What proposals?'

'They imagine that climate change is like a 'disease' that can get worse and has to be stopped by action, like quarantining Covid. They have fastened onto Net Zero, which is an invalid concept, as if demanding it will control the climate, which is impossible.'

'Why impossible?'

'The mechanism of climate warming is not known,' Paul said. 'The supposed Net Zero treatment, ending fossil fuel combustion, may have no effect. It cannot stop climate change everywhere. It would be wiser to treat the symptoms with proven technology, known to reduce climate warming, such as conservation of energy by reduction in emissions of energy. The warming is from human energy use and much of it is wasted energy.

'For myself, I have chosen to reduce my energy consumption and I am reducing my consumption of meat. My sacrifices go unrecognised because the government is captivated by a false prophecy. They want electricity users to pay more, not use less .

'Here is a diagram comparing the four different strategies.

LIKELY RESPONSE TO TREATMENT CHOICE		INDIVIDUAL	
		ACTION	NO ACTION
OTHERS	ACTION	1. Net Zero reduces warming but doesn't stop it.	2. Individual maverick stigmatised for freeloading
	NO ACTION	3.Personal sacrifices with energy and meat reduction martyrdom.	4. Uncontrolled risk of inaction

'Strategy #1 has the government shutting down coal power stations assuming renewable energy will be available. Others will continue to operate them, with pollution continuing. #2 has me as a maverick free-loader who would keep burning fossil fuels, suffering any pollution risk, declining to join the herd and accepting their pollution. #3 has me pioneering personal sacrifice of electricity use. #4 is inaction by everyone, which the government cannot consider because it is supposed to act.'

'Do you think you can oppose all the momentum that has built up?' the interviewer asked.

'My views attract anarchists and a few stoics,' Paul said. 'In time, the futility of Net Zero will become apparent. The benefits of the Net Zero action are so geographically diverse and difficult to discern, their presence will seem to be only theoretical, for a very long time. The proponents of the strategy will gradually lose confidence. On the other hand, my sacrifices can have immediate effects. Although they are non-conforming, they are probably more valuable than those made by herd members.'

'Has the Government staked too much on reducing carbon emissions?' the interviewer asked.

'Yes. The nanny state's popularity demands action, but the outcome could be disappointing. My supporters can offer an alternative to action that could be stigmatised as freeloading, but could reduce climate change by other means.'

The interviewer thanked him and left. A transcript of the interview was published verbatim in a news article online. The Net Zero strategy continued to be hotly debated.

Chapter 28 Federal Election

An election of representatives to Parliament was announced by the Prime Minister to take place in three months' time. There would be election of MPs to the lower house and election of half the senate seats in the upper house.

Voting for the senate would be for candidates either in a party or as individuals. Paul did not explore the rigmarole of preferential vote counting, beyond being determined to be counted as an independent individual. There could have been opportunities to band with other independents as a party, but he wasn't interested.

His campaign was modest. It seemed to him to be wrong that candidates in a gang could command much more attention from advertisers, donors and subscribers. In his view, a political representative should obtain support from his constituency, without ganging up with others in a party, enabling him to gain attention and funds.

Media comment on his candidature usually fixed on his independent status. He explained to reporters that he opposed the nanny state's rampant legislation favouring growth in State provision of services, including free acupuncture. He planned to persuade parliament to allow the public the freedom, services and the privacy they had enjoyed in the past, with the exception of a couple of items where legislation was justified.

He limited his campaigning to door-knocking, public meetings and blogging online.

The people who came to their doors were usually interested in his independent campaign, although it could have been politeness that kept them questioning him. It took time for contact to be meaningful and he reached only a small part of the constituency.

He held several public meetings in local halls. He spoke about local development and the future of the suburb. He was asked his view of provision by the two major parties and he replied that blanket nanny state provision was wasteful and often unwanted. Planning should be local and party intrusion was not wanted.

His online advertising on his blog received encouraging comments. Social media, instead of promoting political debate, prevented it by declining to post controversies.

Facebook and other platforms accepted material that would stimulate responses without upsetting entrenched followers. Due to their censorship, there was no debating. They should allow free speech and if people were offended, they could read something else.

Polling day was fine weather and a high compulsory turnout was expected. It took 3 days to count the votes and apply the preferences.

The returning officer announced he was elected, as the only independent Queensland senator in the 76 seat parliament. The main parties had it sewn up and he didn't receive any offers to side with them, not that he would have accepted any.

In Canberra, he was sworn in and took his seat on the cross bench as the lone independent senator. He returned to Brisbane when he could, between sittings and for long weekends.

His work in the Senate was concerned with refugees and asylum seekers. Investigating the government position took a lot of time with the overall aim of controlling immigration. It was difficult to deal with residency applications fairly without stimulating boat arrivals. But most of my time was taken advising constituents petitioning for favourable immigration treatment by the nanny state.

Chapter 29
Referendum

After winning the federal election, the Labour Party kept its promise to hold a referendum to change the constitution, creating a Voice for Indigenous people in the new parliament. It was an instance of government hubris and overreach, because not enough of the people seemed likely to support it, far short of the majority needed. The Government hoped that public discussion and debate would win people over.

The parties began putting the case for Yes and No votes in a referendum to be held in several months' time. Media interest in The Voice referendum seemed intended to promote conflict. Documentation was as follows.

What you'll be voting on:

i. there shall be a body, to be called the Aboriginal and Torres Strait Islander Voice;

ii. the Aboriginal and Torres Strait Islander Voice may make representations to the Parliament and the Executive Government of the Commonwealth on matters relating to Aboriginal and Torres Strait Islander peoples;

iii. the Parliament shall, subject to this Constitution, have power to make laws with respect to matters relating to the Aboriginal and Torres Strait Islander Voice, including its composition, functions, powers and procedures.

Paragraph i would legitimate an Aboriginal and Torres Strait Islander Voice as a body, having a domain and legislation.

Paragraph ii sought support for Aboriginal and Torres Strait Islander peoples as a separate group, establishing a domain with its own federal nanny.

Paragraph iii required Parliament to separately legislate to establish an Aboriginal and Torres Strait Islander Voice, within its own domain.

The Voice would formalise a role of government, not unlike the 'nanny state', to apply to Aboriginal and Torres Strait Islanders only. A difference was that the nanny state's authority was deduced from its domain in Common Law, whereas the Voice would establish a separate domain in law for a body known as The Voice.

Paul's opposition became well known. He asked the government questions from the floor of the Senate and explained his position. He seemed to be in bed with the Liberal opposition, but remained faithful to his beliefs that Indigenous people already had representation in Parliament and if they were allowed additional representation it was affirmative action that elsewhere would be regarded as discriminatory.

The referendum would be compulsory. The nanny state aligned neither with the Voice, nor against it. Whereas indigenous people obtained benefits from the nanny state, racism was not apparent either way. Indigenous people who were disgruntled were expected to vote for the Voice. It was expected that the indigenous business of the parliament would be transacted by the Voice and this was a sticking point for No! voters who wanted one parliament, not two.

The nanny state had taken over middle Australia as common ground between political parties espousing British, European and American ideas. Our democracy was solid and Australian society was held together by trust, even between communists and libertarians. Their differences could be resolved satisfactorily, without guns or insurrection.

Images of Aborigines making demands filled the media space with a Spectacle that dismayed those who wanted public policy making to be conducted peacefully. They were not reassured that the spiritual sovereignty came from an enduring indigenous sovereignty that co-existed with the sovereignty of the Crown. The referendum was presented divisively without attention to the aftermath of a No vote, nor reconciliation.

The Voice referendum raised the nanny state to an unfamiliar national stage, expected to represent the needs of indigenous people who had been sidelined previously. The Referendum had created a democracy and representation of internal groups and adopted a new rhetorical position.

It seemed hypocritical that the Voice referendum would give Aborigines a voice when the Australian Constitution distinguished Aboriginal Australians and was not being amended to take out this racism.

About 60% of votes were No, not nearly enough to succeed. Australians did not want appointment of a nanny for Aborigines and Torres Straits Islanders. It would fracture the existing nanny state held together by compulsory voting. Voters felt threatened by splitting off a part that was vocal but lacking the leadership needed for cohesion and stability.

Policies of affirmative action were deeply unpopular because they had been tried previously with prejudice ongoing. There were laws preventing discrimination and until these would be enforced, racial prejudice would not be made to disappear by changing the political structure.

The referendum failed because consequences of a Yes vote were feared. Non-compulsory voting could have given a better indication of actual support for more indigenous representation but it is doubtful that there would have been enough voices to endorse rule by an indigenous nanny.

The dust had not yet settled on The Voice referendum and indigenous people were looking for a new way forward. The Nanny States could be called upon to implement land rights and other claims and a federal position could be demanded. State nannies could find their authority challenged and states picked off until the rights of indigenous people were addressed in Federal Law. It could take a long time.

CHAPTER 30 WELCOME TO COUNTRY

The Australia, New Zealand and United States Security Treaty, or ANZUS, was an agreement signed in 1951 to protect the security of the Pacific. Member nations could request assistance from each other.

Australian governments liked to play a leading role in regional affairs without being drawn into regional politics or opposing the USA. It avoided taking a position in any conflict that could adversely affect defence or trade.

The attempt to separate Indigenous representation failed to secure sufficient community support in the referendum. It is relevant that most referenda have failed. The alternative was for political parties to put their proposals to voters during elections.

An alternative is for proposals to be considered with other legislation, but changes to the constitution like The Voice do not qualify. Another is for an indigenous Nanny State to have a greater part in parliamentary democracy, with matters decided by partisan debate rather than enacting multi-party proposals and whole-of-government decisions.

The Voice referendum had not invoked ANZUS, although the USA had provision for separate treatment of indigenous people, allowing groups land where they could develop casinos for revenue. This provision had not been proposed for Australia's indigenous people.

While many people think that a Referendum in 1967 gave Aboriginal and Torres Strait Islander peoples the right to vote, this wasn't the case. Full voting rights were not granted federally until Aboriginal and Torres Strait Islander people were required to register on the electoral roll in 1984.

In 1976 Māori and Cook Islander dancers refused to perform in Western Australia without a welcoming ceremony. A Welcome to Country protocol was adopted, in which 3.8% of the Australian population made token obeisance to the other 96.2%. The welcome could revive animosities lingering for 200 years since the invasion and settlement of Australia by Europeans. The welcome could be construed as setting the stage for weakening of the invaders' tenure and inviting claims for reparation. In 2023, 16.2% of Australia's land area was owned or controlled by Aboriginal and Torres Strait Islander people. Not everyone regarded the welcoming as neighbourly.

Australia has an indigenous Spectacle, with images of Aborigines on their own land. The Spectacle has steadily gathered strength. When the new national government allied itself with a proposal for a referendum on representation of Aborigines and Torres Strain Islanders, there was opportunity for a nanny state Spectacle to support the Yes vote.

The federal nanny's territory is not inherently peaceful. It is riven by identity politics, thriving on conflict, with cultures cancelled by political striving to find support from voters under the sway of party and religious trolls.

Public discourse where the nanny is represented is generated by the Spectacle, whose audiences support political careers with votes and corporate leaders with profits. De Bord characterized the workers Marx had described as alienated, as stay-at-home-TV-watching couch potatoes. Australia's population was moderately alienated by the Voice proposal when it became a political football game between shock jocks, trolls and disaffected Aborigines. The Spectacle of white politicians in vigorous verbal dispute with Australian Aborigines did not reassure anyone that the change would improve relations. The Australian people were compelled to vote and they voted against The Voice, partly from apathy and partly from belief that the status quo should be maintained.

The travesty of the referendum was that it was focussed on a population with 3% aboriginals, when local disparities and practical solutions needed a local focus. The Welcome to Country ceremony exacerbated the rift.

Chapter 31 Social Treatments

Now that he was a senator, Paul had many constituents seeking nanny state social treatments. During the Covid pandemic, the State government had become bogged down with a backlog of individuals needing state care in prisons, detention facilities, asylums, orphanages, foster homes, adoptions, sheltered workshops, special schools, disabled care, nursing homes, hospitals for mentally ill, retirement homes and aged care. Supervision and care of inmates and their rehabilitation required public scrutiny. Paul was assigned by Senate supervisory bodies to inspect facilities.

In addition to evaluation of the progress of each case from within the system, patients, relatives, or care-workers could complain and make demands from outside. There was chronic underfunding of the National Disability Insurance Scheme (NDIS) provision of accommodation and services with complaints about overreach, overprotection and under provision. Because of his interest in nanny state provision, his views on government overreach were well known and he was contacted by patients and families requesting assistance to obtain fair treatment for loved ones. Requests for release were less common.

Paul's response to these complaints was to determine what was happening and to bring it to the attention of the responsible authority. Sometimes that was all that was needed, but he became involved in explaining situations to complainants and working out how difficulties could be overcome. This work was time consuming and senators usually didn't get involved. He became known for his critical eye on welfare of patients in nanny state facilities, particularly from the point of view of overprovision. He was invited to serve on boards of several institutions and he was honoured to accept.

He had run for the Senate under his banner KEEP OUT THE NANNY STATE'. Now his time was taken helping the nanny state to intervene fairly.

Chapter 32 A New Game

Paul had been aware for several years that the nanny state was intruding into public enjoyment of games of rugby football and he complained to the association, but without effect.

He had been a keen player of social rugby but hung up his boots when he turned 35. He bought season tickets to interstate and international games at Ballymore in Brisbane, going with his wife. The games continued their togetherness, that had commenced when they first met at a rugby club party.

At Ballymore they had usually parked and walked to the grandstand, passing vehicles with their open boots laden with food for family picnics. When Pacific Islanders were visiting, the pre-match silence was overhung by gentle mellow voices harmonising with passion in the grandstand,

'Why are they singing?' his wife had asked him.

'I don't know,' he replied. 'Perhaps they are happy?'

'They could be excited and singing to let off steam.'

The grandstand was old and their seats were the same as in previous seasons. Neighbouring seats had been occupied by people they knew. They had chatted during the intervals.

He couldn't remember when the game became fully professional. There had been a gradual change in the rules and digital screens were erected on the touch line in front of them, displaying hype and advertisements, with a lot of noise, blocking their view of the playing field. They stopped going to the games.

Sport was taken up by the nanny state in a big way, with consideration of proposals for rules changes, control of players on and off the field, transfers between clubs, uniform attire, television rights, sponsor promotions, merchandising of bling and media hype, all promoting the Spectacle. Ticket sales to live audiences enabled women's and youth games to reach international audiences.

There were other changes too, with many penalty rulings and players sent off. The games seemed to become relatively tame, with less vigorous physical contact. Once a team's score was ahead, they became defensive. As amateurs they had put their bodies on the line. Now players avoided injury, wanting to collect their pay in the next game.

Another change was that television cameras were there and the players became entertainers. Audiences demanded nail-biting scores and drama. Loose play and scrums had set pieces with a plethora of rules, under the control of the referee, intended to create fairness but slowing down play. Faked injuries and penalty goals were often decisive, making for good television but boring games. The referee blew up infractions and required scrums and lineouts to be repeated many times, until he was satisfied that players were observing the rules. Impartiality of the refereeing determined players' and fans enjoyment of the game.

The referee was an official authorised by the nanny state, serving the audience at the expense of many players who wanted more freedom. Rules limited tackling, bleeding injuries and fighting. There were always tussles, banter, joshing and knuckle sandwiches. Rugby was a physical game formerly played by farmers' sons, labourers and coal miners for fun. Played by office workers, the professional game became sterile.

When Paul objected to the national rugby authority about rules changes, they said the new rules were wanted by advertisers. They wanted infringements at regular intervals, when they could sell merchandise, food and beer.

He looked forward to international games. Rugby Sevens were played at the end of the season by half-size teams with international television audiences. The play had fewer and smaller scrums, with more open play and less niggle. He watched on television free-to-air, but when payment was demanded, he declined. Watching television couldn't equal the live games he had watched and they became fond memories.

For the lowering of standards, he blamed professionalization and pandering to nanny intervention. The rugby Spectacle had once appealed to audiences of male players, but they had been displaced by fans impressed by charisma, physique and athleticism, appealing to females as well as males.

Growth of rugby as a spectator sport was controlled by the rugby associations and the media. Paul wanted more involvement than watching from an armchair, with the atmosphere of amateurism and fun that ruled in Sevens' competitions. Fans' expectations were fostered by advertising and spruiking. Television audiences learned more about goods advertised than about the rugby contest.

North Americans are deterred from serious interest in rugby by the asymmetry of the ball and the absence of protective head and body gear. When he had played, after every game a contingent had lined-up in the hospital for X-rays of suspected fractures. There had been an element of pride in sacrificing one's body, as if it was a macho pursuit, esteemed by fans. Gridiron enthusiasts found rugby chaotic. They admired carefully orchestrated plays whereas in rugby spontaneity dominated.

His concern was that all the hype and hoopla surrounding games should not detract from player performances. If it did, audience numbers would soon dwindle. The nanny state sought to capitalize on the Spectacle and overlooked the traditions of the games. Paul was not alone in voicing these concerns but the organisers replied that the new rules were bringing record earnings. The new game was making more money.

CHAPTER 33 TOWARDS FREEDOM

The nanny state had sometimes provided new opportunities but always reduced personal freedom. People were often unaware of the freedom they had lost. Paul wanted them to choose lifestyles offering real freedom, that preserved the rights and well-being of others.

Freedom! had been the rallying cry of democracy in revolutionary France, the USA and Cuba. He hoped to persuade voters that by electing him they would have a representative who would lead senators from narrow partisanship to endorsement of real freedoms.

John Stuart Mill (24) exhorted citizens to seize liberty while respecting others' rights. Mill's respect for others, when seizing freedom, was a big ask but it was an ideal that had survived in politics. His pledge was refreshed by Hannah Arendt in her book The Origins of Totalitarianism (4). For her, freedom was to be sought and cherished, not chosen among a set of possible alternatives, but with spontaneity, i.e. *the capacity to begin, to start something new, to do the unexpected, with which all human beings are endowed by virtue of being born.*

Nelson Mandela (25) invoked an exterior culture of freedom:

'For to be free is not merely to cast off one's chains, but to live in a way that respects and enhances the freedom of others.'

Ayn Rand was more cavalier about the interior of freedom:

'Our ultimate freedom is the right and power to decide how anybody or anything outside ourselves will affect us.'

Her critics found her freedom intelligent, but arrogant and condescending.

Paul wanted freedom that was a complex spectacle of these images, that changed with the public policy context. His fight against the Nanny State was ongoing but his burden was becoming easier to bear with familiarity. His campaign against the nanny state was intended to free people from the shackles of loyalty to a state that prevented criticism and debate of alternatives. Once the nanny state had declared its position, it was the dominant position and there was seldom debate of alternatives.

Parliamentary business was organised by the government to avoid all but token opposition. Criticism of the nanny state was criticism of the government and was usually pursued by partisan interests which came to the fore at elections. Parties would promise to rescind offensive nanny state legislation when they were elected, but seldom did. Political parties had lost Paul's respect. His loneliness as an independent senator was compensated for by the support of his followers, for whom personal freedom was the core of their belief in democracy.

Chapter 34
Compulsory Voting

As of January 2020, of the 36 member states of the Organisation for Economic Co-operation and Development, only Australia had forms of compulsory voting which were enforced in practice. As of December 2021, 21 countries were recorded as having compulsory voting. Australia is one of ten countries that enforces compulsory voting in political elections. Voting is compulsory in a few countries, but is not enforced.

Australia's nanny state has compulsory voting with governments claiming mandates for their policies, even if they were not included in their platform. The nanny state benefits from voter compliance without its policies receiving voter scrutiny. Although the nanny state is strengthened under compulsory voting, democracy is confounded by the nanny state.

About 90% of enrolled constituents in Australia usually vote, because compulsory voting is maintained by punishing absconders with fines. In Paul's view, requiring enrolled voters to vote was nanny state over-reach.

He was concerned that the electorate was made up of three groups:

1. Respectable, reliable people who could be relied on to vote voluntarily.
2. Flawed people with unreliable opinions who were allowed to vote too.
3. The remainder who don't want to vote and shouldn't be forced to vote.

Compulsory voting was the foundation of government mandate at the heart of Australian parliamentary democracy.

'To obtain unity of purpose, everyone has to vote,' was a popular mantra.

Paul's belief was that whatever the voting system, it should enable a good leader to emerge by unity of purpose, to be obeyed by good followers.

'Not everyone needs to vote,' he said. 'Many voters' consideration of the voting options is cursory. Some couldn't find their way to a bus stop. They accept that they cannot select a leader and want to be loyal followers, but are bullied into casting meaningless unreproducible votes that confuse selection of the leader.

'In the UK, voting is non-compulsory. Voter turnout of 40% is not regarded as disqualification of the elected representatives from forming a stable government and opposition. There was dignity in declining to vote and following the judgement of others.

'Many enrolled voters don't want to vote in an election. They may be disinterested or impartial. Compelling people to vote is harmful.'

A UK government elected by 30% of constituents must obtain support from other parties to have its legislation passed. Its posture must be persuasive. Unless it can conduct government business with majority support, parliament can be dissolved and an election held. To avoid this, it will be careful to secure agreement from opposition parties. The government avoids antagonising electors with unpopular legislation. The Government has to be more prudent.

In Australia, swinging voters are fewer in number and are not able to limit government over-reach by dissolving parliament and calling an election. A government with a compulsory vote of 75% can muster a majority and assume it has a mandate to bully parliament to approve arrogant and self-serving legislation. However much it antagonises the opposition, it is unlikely to face an election for 5 years.

It is concluded that compulsory voting obtains a less adventurous style of government, while encouraging the ruling party to be arrogant. It is likely to run full term, even when a change of government is needed.

Chapter 35 Covid

In 2020 Australia suffered outbreaks of coronavirus. In the early days, before there was experience of controlling it, media were beset by a welter of theories and opinions about the disease.

When I posted an analysis on Facebook, it was rejected 'Not true'. I had statistics. for the increase in hospital deaths per day, showing influenza and pneumonia were ten times higher than from Covid, in Australia from 2017 to 2020. When I presented Facebook references for my sources with the publication details, the fact checkers accepted my post. Had the fact checkers made my analysis available on Facebook without delay, public concern would have been assuaged.

'The nanny state helped manage the Covid outbreak: people became accustomed to being ordered around by the nanny state and did what the Covid authority wanted. Towards the end, public cooperation had crumbled and people chose whether to mask, gather in groups and quarantine.'

'There were demonstrations in Brisbane against mandatory vaccination,' I said.

'Fortunately, common sense prevailed,' said Julia. 'The authorities withheld mandatory vaccination. There was no confrontation with the police.'

The pandemic sputtered on in a few hot spots, but eventually fizzled out. An aftermath was and aged care facilities were overwhelmed and health services were stretched. A residue of authoritarian public health policy-making lingers in 2024.

CHAPTER 36 NOVAVIRUS

A future pandemic of Novavirus can be imagined, similar to Covid. A worldwide novavirus outbreak would bring various Government responses. There would be many theories, without much conclusive testing being done and the consensus in Australia would be that restrictions imposed by the nanny state for Covid would be the best intervention. Other measures such as self diagnosis and treatment would seem radical.

Paul would resist social restrictions, school closures, lockdowns and masking, reflecting his belief that isolated living depressed people and precipitated disease rather than prevented it.

'The longer we go without masks and allow healthy people to encounter the virus, the better will herd immunity strengthen and waylay infection,' he said. 'This is intuitive experience because there was no controlled testing of other alternatives during Covid. 'Public policy would be carried along on a wave of trust.'

'The blind led the blind,' said Julia.

'The nanny state is overreaching,' Paul said. "The efficacy of restrictions has not been determined.'

'You need to rein in your scepticism,' said Julia assertively 'Experience from tracing sources of infection has revealed restrictions were partly successful. There is evidence that lockdowns, hygiene, social distancing, sterilisation and masking had benefits. This could also be inferred from the sharp decline in influenza, which was fortuitously reduced by the Covid restrictions. Models of virus transmission and protection technologies have become more confident.'

'The protection technologies are dubious,' Paul said. 'The assumption that virus infection can be excluded by a mask is misconceived. There can be millions of particles swarming in air, not only penetrating face masks but inhabiting our bodies. When they are numerous they cause infections, unless resisted by immunity. A mask can even cause infection by reducing fresh air intake, reducing oxygen intake and exposing the wearer to higher levels of carbon dioxide. But a mask is effective in stopping spittle, with at least some of the droplets getting onto surfaces and thence into other people.'

'Masking is better than nothing,' Julia said.

'Masking does not give perfect protection and reduces ability to exercise,' Paul said. 'Cringing precautions, lockdowns, partial hygiene and attempts at sterilisation, such as deep cleaning, could be worse than useless. They can reduce our natural immunity, allowing worse virus strains to evolve, weakening our resolve and making us defenceless. Masking is not a panacea and could even be harmful. The nanny state's excessive precautions could induce fear and learned helplessness, increasing infection rates.'

Chapter 37 Elective Surgery

During the Covid pandemic, hospital beds were in short supply. They were allocated by the nanny state with input from hospitals and State political authorities. People wanted to know what was happening but hospital statistics were not transparent.

Hospitals normally offered elective operations, such as appendectomies, at the same time as necessary surgery, such as prostatectomies. Often they were accepted. Due to the shortage of beds for Covid victims, elective surgery had come to a standstill.

Paul served on several hospital boards where priorities for elective surgery were debated. He was generally opposed to unnecessary operations. Medical exploitation with 'machines that go Bing' was satirized in Monte Python's movie *Life of Brian*. The phenomenon of medical wards competing with treatments to raise revenue was potentially real and could not be ignored.

The reverse, with patients unreasonably refusing treatments that would be in their own interests, was less concerning. Patients could not in theory be forced to have any of the following treatments administered by the State: blood transfusion, tonsils, appendectomy, circumcision, adenoids, prostate removal, wisdom teeth extractions, abortion, sterilisation, euthanasia, electro-convulsive therapy. Inessential operations were paid for by Medicare, the nanny state, without quibble.

It was less usual that when medics and hospitals refused, near relatives sought overriding medical approval, such as for female genital mutilation and abortions. Medics were guided by humanitarian reasoning, or by relatives' approvals of circumcisions.

There was a trickle of cases where operations were mandated, by a nanny state, opposing individuals' or near relatives' permissions. Jehovah's Witnesses sometimes refused to have their children receive blood transfusions, loyal to their belief in a Biblical injunction against tissue transfer. Paul believed it was an important precedent for other parents to observe refusal of unnecessary operations on children. For older patients, refusal of euthanasia should be respectable. The important roles of near relatives and permissions for hospital operations were highlighted to increase in importance when these operations would keep loved ones alive.

In Paul's view, the nanny state must honour the treatment wants and beliefs of family and near friends. In most cases, medics and hospitals would agree with them. Respect for the Jehovah's Witnesses' refusal of blood transfusion should be acknowledged, because it was only a short step away to refusing treatment by euthanasia of patients with dementia. Nanny state authorisation of elective medical treatments should be allowed only under exceptional circumstances.

Paul and Julia held a small party with friends to celebrate the end of Covid. Paul made a brief speech.

'This is a party to celebrate our survival and thank each of you for providing support.

'We are fortunate to have muddled through. Now is the time to start planning what we will do next time, for another pandemic is quite likely.

'There is no time like the present for considering what to do' he said. 'Last time, the nanny state's actions were politically expedient but they didn't make much sense from epistemological and scientific viewpoints. I hope our epidemiologists will digest experience in Australia and learning overseas to be better prepared next time. But I am not counting on them for a coherent response to the threat of a similar pandemic.'

'What sort of response are you thinking about?'

'An early response. We could plan our actions in a meeting of this group again at the same time next week.'

'Would we be planning for ourselves, or making a proposal to the State government?'

'That's what we could discuss next week and anything else. For example, if the government's response is inadequate, we could demonstrate our concern with a protest march. We need to decide what we want.'

'Good idea,' said someone. 'I'll come.'

Most of the others agreed to be there too.

Chapter 38
Compulsory Vaccination

A week later the group met again in a more sombre mood. Paul started the proceedings.

'Imagine a future outbreak of Novavirus, similar to Covid. I predict Australian authorities would mandate vaccinations.

'It would extend the arsenal of restrictions the population obeyed during the Covid,' Julia speculated.

'Vaccination cannot be enforced,' Paul said.

'I oppose mandatory Covid vaccination because it could be the thin end of an authoritarian medical treatment wedge. If we accept it, there will be all kinds of other treatments that could be imposed in the future. Already there is a shortage of surgery beds and serious medical conditions are deprioritised.

'Mandatory vaccination would be an abuse of power,' Paul said.

'Compulsory vaccination in the USA almost succeeded during Covid, then it was outlawed,' Julia said. 'We couldn't do it here.'

'The U.S. Supreme Court, in *Jacobson v. Massachusetts*, 197 U.S. 12 (1905) ruled that the State of Massachusetts could compel residents to obtain free vaccination or revaccination against smallpox, or suffer a penalty of $5 (about $150 today) for noncompliance. The court's judgement initially relied on four criteria in deciding to compel vaccination:

1. There was a benchmark minimum number of consequential deaths (set at 500,000 by the defence during later prosecution of the tobacco industry).
2. *The vaccination mandate was not shown to be arbitrary or oppressive.* There were few arbitrary exemptions for those affected and treated, nor for others oppressed by it.

3. Other approved medications were available to reduce transmission of infection.
4. Vaccine safety and efficacy had been established for less than 100 years, (exceeded with the smallpox vaccine).

'The absence of these four conditions made mandatory vaccination unreasonable and therefore illegal during the Covid epidemic,' Paul said. 'None of the four Jacobson criteria are present for Novavirus vaccination in Australia. If the governments of the US or Australia were to proceed with a vaccine mandate, it would be an unwarranted overreach, inconsistent with established public health policy and law (11).'

'Jacobson's criteria were for a different disease, smallpox,' said Julia.

'True; but the epidemiology for vaccination refusal is similar,' Paul replied.

'The Australian nanny state could overrule it,' said Julia. 'They could control the Novavirus pandemic by quarantine, by voluntary vaccination, by reduced socialisation, by social distancing and by voluntary masking, as we experienced in Covid.'

'The nanny state political leaders, ignoring Jacobson, would order the State Government to enact new compulsory vaccination laws. They would order citizens going to work to be vaccinated or to stay at home,' said Paul.

'Those who want protection by vaccinating others should stay at home.'

'Mandatory vaccination would cause panic,' said Michelle. 'People won't be herded by a totalitarian state. The police won't be able to enforce it.'

'They wouldn't succeed in bringing the virus under control,' Paul said. 'It will destroy the economy. We should protest now, before there is chaos.'

They talked together about joining in a protest rally commencing in their local inner-city park, then marching to where parliament was sitting. That evening, the friends and neighbours met in the barbecue area of their apartments, attracting attention with leaflets, phone calls, placards and a billboard on the street.

Chapter 39 Protest Plan

Paul, Julia, Michelle and Chance met to imagine a protest demonstration and plan it.

'The nanny state is ignoring the Jacobson criteria that outlawed mandatory vaccination in the United States. Mandatory restrictions should be illegal,' Paul began. 'We didn't have mandatory vaccination during Covid and there were few deaths.'

Michelle recited the Jacobson criteria.

'We haven't reached those levels yet,' she said. 'They can't enforce vaccination for Novavirus.'

'They will consider enforcing it and we must stop them,' Paul said. 'Will you join me in a protest rally. We don't want an insurrection. We won't be doing more than protesting legally against Government restrictions. We want the restrictions to be withdrawn. Protesting is legal when protesters have a reasonable excuse. Our excuse is that although we have tested negative, our rights to access city streets, public transport and public amenities is prevented by police.

'Forced vaccination is a condition of access to loved ones, or to your workplace. It disrespects individual sovereignty,' he said. 'My body is my temple and access to it is under strict control of my mind or, if I am temporarily unable to function, by my appointed attorney under an advanced health directive.

'Vaccination enforcement is heinous, in the same way as enforcing a lobotomy would be if I become mentally ill. Without legal approval, electro-convulsive therapy is illegal.

Several friends of Julia joined the meeting.

'We shouldn't be challenging laws like 20-year olds,' Paul said. 'We should be putting our energy into our careers and looking for advancement. We should plan now how we will deal with totalitarianism when it arises and get on with our lives. I am prepared to die opposing mandatory restrictions.'

There was silence. People looked at each other.

'Me too!' chimed one of the newcomers loyally.

Michelle held her hand to her mouth and shook her head.

'Hopefully it won't come to that,' she said.

Paul told them of his idea to oppose Government restrictions.

'The Occupation of Brisbane will be an act of nonviolent non-cooperation and civil disobedience. The purpose is to end unjust restrictions that are preventing people pursuing their activities in public places. During Covid, unelected persons imposed arbitrary authority.

I want to resist totalitarian conditions of arbitrary ideology, centralism, dictatorship, atomism, surveillance and tyranny. The government has given itself a legal framework to prevent a popular movement opposing it, preventing gathering, communication and leadership. We have to oppose the government by passive resistance.

'We plan to walk through city streets unvaccinated, not socially distanced, nor masked,' said Michelle. 'If there are enough of us, they will have difficulty stopping us and we can oppose their violence with passive resistance.'

'It's not my aim to be the leader who is opposing the State Government,' Paul said. 'I could be arrested and charged with insurrection. We can take turns at being leaders in this action. Our leadership will be dispersed, in loosely affiliated groups of non-violent dissenters.

'I will walk quietly through city streets ignoring the lockdown. Restrictions of vaccinations and face masks would apply to those who test positive. Others would be able to march freely.

'Mobilising the population will begin the first day' he said. 'The day after, we would display our intention to oppose the Government by walking and rallying. The third day would culminate the protest. We will walk making a legal protest and if the Police try to restrict us we will non-violently oppose the restrictions. We will defy the Police. If we become violent and unarmed protestors are injured we will lose public support. Thousands of protesters will be arrested and they will clog the prisons, refusing to pay the fines, bringing the city to a standstill. The government would have to end restrictions or resign.

'Leave now if you don't want to be a part of this,' Paul said. 'Those who remain, when you go home, prepare to meet again next week when we will plan our protest in detail.

They stayed and discussed their plan so far, agreeing to meet to plan a protest in detail.

CHAPTER 40 WALKING

The group met a week later to plan their protest against imaginary future government restrictions.

Paul posted the notice below on his laptop blog and sent copies to citizens, subscribers and news media.

'Team, this will be my email to launch our demonstration tomorrow.

MEDIA RELEASE

COMMENCEMENT OF PROTEST AGAINST NOVAVIRUS RESTRICTIONS COMMENCES TODAY AT 9.00 AM.

This media release announces an intended Occupation of Brisbane by citizens to protest expected Government Novavirus restrictions: civilians are unable to enter, without proof of vaccination, public buildings and places of employment, subject to employers' requirements. Travel for inessential purposes and to visit family members in residential institutions is also banned; schools are closed.

Demonstrate your rejection of these restrictions by joining our Protest Walk to the city centre TODAY.

'In the USA The Jacobson criteria reveal that vaccination refusal should have grounds for respect and compulsory vaccination is unlawful. Because the restrictions have not had due legal processing in Australia, their implementation by police is 'reasonable excuse' for protest against over-reach by the nanny state. Therefore, this protest demonstration is not illegal.

The protest is now launched and my involvement ceases except as a protester. There is no leader. Tell others to imagine walking and rallying, today, from 10.00am, and again tomorrow at 12 noon.

Signed,

Paul Finething,
Citizen of Brisbane.

'Today we will continue planning the protest demonstration to commence tomorrow.

'The media will announce the commencement, informing our purpose and where people can join in. Walkers will each carry a placard: 'FREEDOM'.

We few at 9.00 am will begin walking from our homes to an arterial road leading to the city centre and Parliament.

Julia showed them her laptop placards they would carry announcing: WE PROTEST NONAVIRUS VACCINATION COMPULSION and: WE CAN GO WHERE WE WANT. They carried a banner: OCCUPY BRISBANE AT 10 AM TODAY AND TOMORROW AT 12 NOON.

'We would be joined by other walkers and by the time the road joined a freeway, there will be several thousand walkers. We would follow a police car with flashing lights and we would spread out and block one side of the highway. We will not seek permission to walk in the road but the Police would be unprepared to stop us. We would proceed like this across a river bridge and into the CBD shopping precinct, where others, alerted by media, would join us. We would rally in Town Hall square, with speeches on megaphones. The atmosphere will be festive: people would be enjoying the sunshine.'

'How many people could there be?' asked Michelle.

'Several thousand will gather in the square for an hour, then we will walk to the State Parliament. There could be tens of thousands from the shopping precinct walking with us.

'When we get to the Parliament we will send in a message requesting to speak with the Premier. We will chant 'STOP THE VACCINATION MANDATE.'

'If the Premier comes out, I will inform him that today is a rehearsal for a mass non-violent demonstration tomorrow, unless the mandatory restrictions are lifted today.

'A journalist with a TV camera would interview our spokespersons, who would be Michelle and Paul, at the entry gate to the parliament building.

'Why are you protesting?' the journalist would ask. 'Wouldn't it be better to cooperate by getting vaccinated and wearing masks?'

'If our right to walk in the street is taken away or weakened,' Michelle answered, 'is it possible that in future we could be sterilised, euthanized, conscripted into the military, aborted, refused abortion, forced to give blood, have our gender changed, have offspring genetically modified, or have a mind-altering mental treatment administered?'

The journalist waited.

'We think the answer is a definite yes,' said Paul. 'Once we accept mandatory conditions, more would follow.

'It is unreasonable to expect people to accept vaccination when they distrust the vaccines and distrust the Government's intent,' Michelle told her. 'The Jacobson criteria show the Government hasn't the right to enforce a mandate that disrespects individuality. The Government is our government and it must allow us freedom. We are not threatening the government: we are disobeying it.'

The Premier won't come out and talk. We will announce the demonstration again next day.

Michelle and Paul would be arrested. They would go passively. Without violence. They would be escorted to a vehicle and driven away to be imprisoned. Julia would get away.

'Tomorrow we will show them we are serious,' said Julia as Paul and Michelle were driven away. They would be locked in separate cells overnight.

Their arrest hardened the marchers' resolve. By the evening of this first day, there were 30,000 walkers obstructing half a dozen roads around Parliament. The protestors stayed talking together about the plan for the next day, until they left to go home.

Chapter 41
Confrontation

Next day, Paul and Michelle would be released from prison, setting off for the city centre together at 12 noon.

'I want to go with you,' Julia would say.

'We need you in support,' Paul would reply. 'We could need help. I'll keep in touch by phone.

They would walk under shady trees through boulevards, beside pedestrians commuting to work and shopping by bicycle, on scooters and on foot. Under the trees, the light was greenish and cool.

Store keepers were boarding up their windows against violence and looting. The police had closed off the city centre and formed lines at barricades across streets, requiring vaccination cards or certificates on phones to be shown for entry.

At 12 noon the protesters would cram into the Town Hall square.

At 1.00pm that would set off as a street-wide column walking towards the Parliament building. When they tried to walk in the City Centre streets without a vaccination certificate, police would tell them to go home.

'Test us for the virus,' Paul would say. 'If we are negative, we have a right to be in a public place.'

Their tests would be negative.

They would walk ahead of a growing horde of all ages, some answering the call to action pushing children in strollers. They wore jeans, shorts and T-shirts, many with slogans. They wore hats against the hot sun and carried water bottles. As they passed shops, offices and factories, workers would pour out on to sidewalks to watch and clap. Many of them joined in.

They chanted: 'WE ARE ONE. WE HAVE THE POWER' and:
'KEEP OUT THE NANNY STATE'
'TESTING IN; VACCINE OUT'

They would step to a sombre drumbeat. People would be angry. It would be concerted forward movement of individuals deliberately choosing non-violent confrontation with authority.

Their phalanx of unvaccinated walkers would come to a wall of helmeted police with riot shields and water cannons. When those at the front were pushed forward from behind, police would club them to the ground. There was shouting and screaming but there would be no retaliation. Those felled and injured would be carried back with broken bones, concussed and bloody, by their friends and laid on the ground where they would be cared for. Others would take their places. The line moved resolutely forward, with vaccinated protesters caught in the crush. The police's checking for vaccination became ineffective. The movement was swollen as bystanders joined in. Wave after wave would push forward and then be beaten down. The street was like a battleground with dozens of bodies. The Police would be unable to deter the walkers. They frenetically arrested and removed them to prison, but the prisons would already be filled to overflowing.

Michelle and Paul avoided attracting attention. They moved forward with the throng. The Government was unable to arrest a leader. Paul was felled with a cut on his head and Michelle's arm broke defending herself against a police attacker.

Paul called Julia. She came and put Michelle's arm in a sling.

'Are we winning?' asked Julia.

'No. They're losing,' said Michelle.

CHAPTER 42 RESOLUTION

The planners expected, after several hours of beating unresisting protesters, the police would become physically exhausted and demoralised as in Ghandi's Salt March in 1930. The city centre would be taken over by the rebels. The jails would be full and still the streets would throng with walkers. By evening, the challenge to Government authority had overwhelmed the Police. They quit their posts and anyone could go to the city centre without being challenged. The Government had lost control.

200,000 protestors were resisting the government passively with civil disobedience. Their resistance on this occasion was not against British rule of the Indian sub-continent, but against Queensland State authority in Australia. It was civil disobedience. Police mutinied from their brutal task of opposing non-violence. They would fear the determination of the protestors and desert their posts.

Worldwide media attention would be on the occupation of Brisbane. The focus of protest would be lockdown of a City that had mandated vaccination for entry to workplaces. It had been overcome by unvaccinated citizens who, when they had tested negative, demanded access to their places of employment.

The people would rise in revolt. Before the Occupation of Brisbane, the nanny state had been steadily gaining power, taking away self-determination. The spectacle had pandemic images of medical chaos and catastrophic death, converting these into profits. Investment for profit was helped by government funding and a fearful populace, creating expensive vaccines, quarantine facilities, treatment technologies, construction of hospitals, unpopular restrictions and welfare handouts. The protestors would have support at home from citizens who would reject the discredited Spectacle. It was the effectiveness of the protestors non-violent opposition to mandatory vaccination that would cause restrictions to be withdrawn and the Government to resign.

The conflict was between those who tried to assert a right to be protected from the virus, by stopping others' rights to travel, to work and preventing engagement in activities in the public space. A silent minority wanted to be absolutely protected, as if this were possible, by mandating exclusion of potentially infectious persons. But the Government was unable to act for the cautious 'haves' against the reckless and anarchistic 'have-nots' who threatened insurrection because their exclusion would mean loss of their livelihoods.

Michelle and Paul would stay up all night, bandaging and supporting protestors and modelling peaceful behaviour. The police would carefully avoid clashing with them. The Government would backdown, making all restrictions voluntary. It was a victory for individualism. Widespread infection was forecast but many people were protected by their vaccinations. Vaccinations could be required by businesses, schools and hospitals, but people who tested negative, even without a vaccination certificate, could not be excluded.

Unvaccinated people would be urged to self-test and self-quarantine if necessary. A vigorous programme of tracing and testing at outbreaks would avert spreading. Hiding of unvaccinated persons in the vaccinated herd was prevented by requiring non-compliant individuals to display negative vaccination status visibly with an X.

Peace would emerge when the Government lifted their ineffective lockdown and focussed on maintaining order on the streets but cancelled the vaccination mandate. State leaders realised that transgression of free rights of the majority was a much more serious problem than protection from Novavirus of a small part of the population. Control on the streets would be lost, Police would quit, outnumbered and humbled. The Government would resign.

The protesters would overcome the learned helplessness of the nanny state. Non-violence would prevail.

Non-violence is the greatest force at the disposal of mankind. It's mightier than the mightiest weapon of destruction devised by the ingenuity of man.
Mahatma Gandhi

Nanny state totalitarianism would be thwarted. Individualism would be asserted. The government, which had been intent on levelling, had used the pandemic as an excuse to charge headlong towards totalitarianism, until the protestors opposed them. Besides preventing mandatory vaccination, the protestors would restore social gatherings and reopen schools. A temporary coalition government would take over, to keep law and order, with capitalism held back on a short leash of public good.

They would defy the National Government and its rule of fear.

CHAPTER 43 STATE ELECTION

After planning their Protest Walk, they continued in their jobs knowing what to do if there was another pandemic. They would not succumb to the fear and superficial policy-making experienced with Covid. Their non-violent resistance would replace the authoritarian government with a temporary coalition government.

A four-yearly State election was due in three months and the politicians divided into partisan camps. There was the usual bickering and infighting.

The State election took place and the liberal coalition took a majority of 45% with labour getting 30%. Their vaccination policy failure had lost labour the election. The new government claimed to have a mandate for its election policies of public transport expansion and renewal of the electricity supply system.

'After the turmoil of Covid, it's good to get back to infrastructure matters,' Michelle said.

'I hope the government can serve the public without using the money to attract votes,' Paul said. 'The nanny state is on the back foot and that's where she should stay.'

'The pushing forward of the nanny state to act as a scape goat has to end,' said Michelle.

'Our politicians will need to accept more responsibility.'

CHAPTER 44 NANNY PARLIAMENT

Paul stayed in Brisbane and went to the first session of the new Queensland State Parliament. He asked Andrea if she would like to go with him.

'It's a school day,' she said. 'What would I see?'

'You'll see how laws are made. The Queensland Parliament has many procedures and rules like the Federal Senate where I work. I'm a visitor here and I want to see if they work as hard as we do in Canberra. We'll only stay until Lunch Break. Then you can go to school.'

'Okay,' she said. 'If it's boring, I'll read a book.'

They sat together in the Public Gallery.

Paul showed Andrea a copy of the schedule.

Source: Queensland State Parliament Schedule of Sessions (23).

Tuesday Wednesday Thursday

Tuesday

From 9.30 am to 10.15 am Preliminary Business

Prayers.

There were many brief notices.

There was a message from the Governor, acting for the Monarch.

'What's happening?' Andrea asked. 'What are all these people doing?'

'Those seated are mostly elected members. They are here representing the people in their constituencies who elected them. First they are planning who will do what. Then they will start the business and the leaders say what the government is doing and what it should do.'

'Why are they talking about it?' Andrea asked her father.

'It's their job.'

'Do they do their jobs well?' she asked. 'Many of them don't seem to be doing anything. Are they bludging?'

'Maybe a few are. There are TV cameras so that the people who voted for them can see what they are doing.'

'If they don't do what they are supposed to, could they lose their seats?'

'Yes, it can happen.'

10.15 am – 11.15 am Question Time

Most of the questions asked whether the government was aware of certain events, seeming to contradict government policies.

Questions are 'without notice' or 'on notice'. The former constitute the whole hour of question time and may contain an element of surprise, since the Government can only speculate on the types of questions without notice that an opposition member might ask. The latter are submitted on paper in the Chamber and are processed by the parliament's Table Office to appear on the next day's Notice Paper. Under the parliament's 'Sessional Orders', ministers are allowed up to 30 days in which to reply. The question and its answer are later published in the parliament's 'Record of Proceedings'.

'I don't understand,' said Andrea.

'They are the rules for asking and answering questions,' said Paul. 'Most members think they are fair. I don't understand the rules either.'

Question time is one hour with speakers in the sequence agreed by the Speaker in consultation with the Whips. Some questions are taken on notice. Questions without notice reiterate policies and events, with interjections from the opposition. Questioning of the opposition is designed to embarrass them.

'Why are they laughing?' Andrea asked.

'The government has been embarrassed by a question and they are trying to save face.'

11.20 am – 1.00pm Government business was heard.

From 1.00 pm to 2.00 pm Lunch Break

From 2.00 pm to 3.00 pm Private members' statements

From 3.00pm to 5.30 pm there was Government Business.

From 5.30 pm to 7.00 pm Disallowance Motions, Private Members; Bills
From 7.00 pm to 8.30 pm Government Business
From 8.30 pm to 9.00 pm Automatic Adjournment

At 11.15 am Government Business was reading of a bill proposing a new Business Development Authority to assist businesses with finance.

Paul was impressed that the new government was getting straight down to business.

As they listened to Barker, Minister for Business Development, Paul felt privileged to live in a place where government policies were presented politely and received courteously, with the exception of occasional calling out by the opposition and admonishment by the speaker.

He recalled their protest march two months earlier, with the police beating him. Since then there had been an election and today he was hearing a new government. The past events had occurred following the rules of the democracy, all except the clubbing of protestors by the police. Again, he felt grateful that there had been a smooth return to parliamentary rule.

He didn't listen to Minister Barker's speech, except his volume, tone, vocabulary and rhythm. He recognised that some of the phrases were meant to win the approval of his side, with occasional insults to the Opposition.

Minister Barker was confident and eloquent. The matter was familiar to him, as it had come from his own office. He didn't expect much opposition despite the Bill favouring Government voters with only a secondary benefit of jobs for Opposition voters.

Paul doubted the reading of this bill would be the high point of Barker's political career. He dozed. Several members were asleep at their benches. Andrea dozed too. It had been a leisurely flow of words and he hadn't noticed any contention other than some heckling at the start.

'If only governing was always this easy,' he thought. His job would be a doddle, if passion and dissension could be omitted.

The listeners began to fidget as the one hour time limit approached.

And then it was done.

Barker's explanatory speech had lasted 1 hour.

Members' first reading had no time for debate.

Andrea left to go to school.

'That was interesting, granddad,' she said politely. 'Bye.'

A second reading debate, on another day, would have 30 minutes from the Minister.

Then other members would have 3 minutes on each question, 10 minutes total.

Finally, the Minister in reply would have 20 minutes and no limit in detail.

The bill had to be checked and could then go forward to a Vote and, if successful, to enactment.

The members went out for Lunch Break.

He reflected on the type of bills that would impose the nanny state on people. The least intrusive government actions nurtured jobs, businesses, infrastructure and offices rather than imposing directly on individuals. They allowed investments which would benefit employers and enterprises initially, rather than workers, because they lacked capital and organisation. For example, construction of a road, marketplace, port, stadium, or a building, could benefit a large group, without creating dependencies. The nanny state could provide facilities that otherwise would not be afforded. Public investment impacted the economy, with the potential to lubricate interaction and harmonise individual effort.

Other bills benefitted the public. The nanny state regulated health services, welfare assistance and safety of a community, it lifted the standard of living of many individuals. New regulations could disadvantage some people, resulting in criticism of the nanny state. Citizens needed to have their say so that a balanced nanny role could be negotiated, with due attention to the greatest good of the greatest number. Until a change was made, many people were not aware they could stop it and the nanny's authority needed to be flexible.

When a pejorative 'nanny state' call was heard, it usually criticised a proposal or a new regulation. Often the critics' objections were considered and the change reversed or modified. When people continued to suffer, the nanny may deem this to be the lesser of evils that people had to put up with. Consequently, the disadvantage should be weighed against others' advantage. However, when there was imposition, nanny state over-reach may need to be curbed.

Later the bills would be debated. The Government would want their proposal of investment in business facilities carried. The opposition would want the money to be spent supporting their investment in training and hiring of health workers to continue.

Paul was a decentralist who wanted businesses to use the government's money to expand their businesses and hire more workers. The difference was that workers had to compete for something the Opposition would hand them on a plate. Investment in business would probably impact sooner on employment than investment in workforce training.

Paul's view was derived from De Bord's Spectacle, in which the workers were alienated from their work and participated passively as spectators. Perhaps the Government couldn't make any difference. He was thankful that the Queensland Parliament was keeping to the time-honoured processes. It was partisanship that ruined it.

He would return to Canberra and his Senate job, happy that his planning to oppose the Queensland Government may not have been noticed. The new Queensland Parliament had yet to reveal whether it would be autocratic and mandate the vaccinations that Paul and his friends had planned to protest.

Chapter 45 Nanny Care

States are supposed to set a framework in which people can live peacefully together. Governments around the world have been inclined to go beyond this traditional role. Instead of issuing some basic rules for collaborating, they try to prescribe specific ways of life, such as socialism. Can these ever be justified, or are government nannies just infantilizing our society?

Does the nanny state's attention to domestic violence merely bring state intervention into private disputes, with a female victim bias? Could the nanny state have intervened earlier, before the resort was to violence?

Another situation with nanny over-reach was building approval for community title dwellings. In Paul's experience, it was hopeless. His plan for a Constructivist College had been bogged down by nanny state over-regulation.

The nanny state in Queensland would not deal with indigenous matters separately. State control of health, safety and the economy was a higher priority.

Paul supported some regulations but opposed others believing freedom had to come from within. Resisting the nanny state was not a popular movement but the number of his supporters was growing. The Government could achieve equal or better social aims by investing in infrastructure and business.

Politicians thought twice before imposing new regulations, putting through rules that would be popular and withholding measures that would disadvantage many. The nanny state in Queensland would not want to allow minorities to benefit at the expense of the majority.

The problem with the nanny state was over-reach resulting from partisan politics.

A viewpoint of party democracy was that a framework was necessary to include a wide range of local experience, able to select popular leaders, who could take actions necessary for the well-being of many of the people. A non-partisan government could achieve an equal or better result without the hype and conflict of adversarial party interaction. Partisan politics glues together policies into nanny state party platforms having over-protection and over-reach.

There used to be a belief that partisan politics would create better government. The philosopher Hegel regarded policy as derived from a dialectical cycle of thesis, antithesis and synthesis. It mobilised the Westminster system with discourse between government and opposition, but debates have become media spectacles. Creative debating has almost disappeared. Nanny state regulation has taken over.

The party system prevents good communication. Most parliamentary business, of considering alternatives, joining factions and voting, could be arranged at online meetings between members. Such a change was unlikely to be welcomed however, because necessary changes in jobs and pay would follow and would clash with partisan members' ambitions. Members wanted to keep their jobs in political parties. It was not a sufficient reason to remain stuck with an antiquated system of government. Authority and a process for reforming Australian government, were badly wanted. The State nanny had to be prevented from taking over.

Paul's campaign to keep out the nanny state added an extra criterion for public approval: absence of opposition by those who would be adversely affected, or who regarded nanny protection with antipathy, as unnecessary, harmful or even with hatred.

Under the system he proposed, too much opposition sounded a knell for many proposals. The result was empowerment of citizens. Public policy entered a new golden age of constructive criticism and creativity.

State investment took over private investment, which had adopted a posture of requiring careful scrutiny and rationalisation of proposals. The words 'nanny state' became praise rather than criticism, a new gold standard for public investment.

'It's nanny state,' Julia said, responding to a government proposal.

'That's good!' said Paul. 'I presume the proponents are entitled to protection, for some reason?'

'Correct. They're risking their careers.'

'Doesn't everyone?'

'Not like this. They're teachers joining the Constructivism College we proposed. They will be quitting safe teaching jobs, without prospect of more improved financial reward.'

'Teaching what you believe in is its own reward.'

'True, but it's not enough to live on. The nanny state needs to intervene for it to be a success.'

'I agree. Nanny state support is needed. The price of government support used to be rigid conformance to regulations, but not anymore.'

'Now every proposal is special, because we know what has to be protected and what over-reach to avoid.'

'The problem is Australia's nanny state has grown too large to be carried within our existing democracy.'

BIBLIOGRAPHY AND REFERENCES

1. Knox, M P, Time is Gold, Novel Ideas, 2020.
2. Knox, M P, Brisbane River Anti-Memoir, 2023.
3. Brymer, G. E., 'Extreme Dude: A Phenomenological Perspective on the Extreme Sport Experience', PhD thesis, Wollongong, 2005.
4. Arendt, H. The Origins of Totalitarianism, 1951
5. De Beauvoir, S. The Ethics of Ambiguity, 1947
6. Vonnegut, K, Harrison Bergeron
7. Persig, R. Zen and the Art of Motorcycle Maintenance, 1974
8. Tyler Brule, Monocle, 2015
9. De Tocqueville, Alexis de, Tocqueville, Alexis de, 1805–1859, Democracy in America.
10. Foucault, M. Nietzsche, Genealogy, History, in D F Bouchard, Ithaca: Cornell University Press, 1977, p153
11. Foucault, M. Discipline and Punish, 1975
12. COVID-19 Vaccine Mandates Fail the Jacobson Test, Epoch Times, December 30, 2021.
13. Nietzsche, F. Thus Spake Zarathustra. 1883
14. Burns, P. 'Albert Einstein's Theory of Happiness', Medium, November 12, 2021
15. De Bord, G, The Society of the Spectacle, 1967
16. Mark Fisher.s Marxist Supernanny, https;//youtu.be/F2GPXGsS
17. McLuhan, M. Understanding Media, 1964
18. Fisher, M. Capitalist Realism – Is there no Alternative?, 2009
19. Knox, M. Turkeys Not Bees, 2022.
20. Seligman, M. Learned Optimism, 1991

21. Durant, W and A, The Lessons of History, Simon & Schuster, 1968
22. Chau, JY; Kite, J, Ronto R; Bhatti, A; and Bonfigliolii, ' Talking about a nanny nation: investigating the rhetoric framing public health debates in Australian news media.' Public Health Res Pract 2019, 29(3): e2931922.
23. Queensland Parliament, Procedures, Sessional Orders of the Legislative Assembly, August 20, 2024
24. John Stuart Mill, 'On Liberty, A System of Logic, The Subjection of Women, and Utilitarianism.'
25. Mandela, Nelson Long Walk to Freedom, 1994.

Available at:
https://www.amazon.com.au/Turkeys-Not-Bees-Martin-Knox/dp/0648993043

www.ingramcontent.com/pod-product-compliance
Lightning Source LLC
Chambersburg PA
CBHW070400200726
48294CB00003B/1007